C000149388

Emily Harvale lives in
although she would pre
Alps...or Canada...or anywhere that has several
months of snow. Emily loves snow almost as much
as she loves Christmas.

Having worked in the City (London) for several
years, Emily returned to her home town of
Hastings where she spends her days writing. And
wondering if it will snow.

You can contact her via her website, Twitter,
Facebook or Instagram.

There is also a Facebook group where fans can
chat with Emily about her books, her writing day
and life in general. Details are on the 'For You'
page of Emily's website.

Author contacts:
www.emilyharvale.com
www.twitter.com/emilyharvale
www.facebook.com/emilyharvalewriter
www.instagram.com/emilyharvale

***

Scan the code above to see all Emily's books on
Amazon

Also by this author:

Highland Fling
Lizzie Marshall's Wedding
The Golf Widows' Club
Sailing Solo
Carole Singer's Christmas
Christmas Wishes – Two short stories
A Slippery Slope
The Perfect Christmas Plan – A novella
Be Mine – A novella
***

The Goldebury Bay series:
Book One – Ninety Days of Summer
Book Two – Ninety Steps to Summerhill
Book Three – Ninety Days to Christmas
***

The Hideaway Down series:
Book One – A Christmas Hideaway
Book Two – Catch A Falling Star
Book Three – Walking on Sunshine
Book Four – Dancing in the Rain
***

Hall's Cross series
Deck the Halls
The Starlight Ball

It Takes Two

Emily Harvale

ISBN 978-1-909917-25-5

Published by Crescent Gate Publishing

Print edition published worldwide 2017
E-edition published worldwide 2017

Editor Christina Harkness

Cover design by JR, Luke Brabants and Emily Harvale

This book is dedicated to all my friends, old and new, who have helped me through a rather trying, seven months of this year. Thank you for being there for me. Thank you for being my friends. It's humbling to know such wonderful people. xx

Acknowledgements

My grateful thanks go to the following:

Hastings Borough Council – planning department. Thank you for answering all my questions regarding planning applications and for explaining the ins and outs of pre-planning meetings. Should I ever wish to build a housing development, I'll know exactly what to do.

The RYA and British Canoeing Organisation. I once belonged to a rowing club in Putney but things have changed a lot since then. Thanks for telling me everything I needed to know, whether or not it appears in this book.

Christina Harkness for her patience and care in editing this book.

My webmaster, David Cleworth who does so much more than website stuff.

My cover design team, JR.

Luke Brabants. Luke is a fabulous artist and can be found at: www.lukebrabants.com

My wonderful friends for their support and friendship. You know I love you all.

My Twitter and Facebook friends, and fans of my Facebook author page. It's great to chat with you. You help to keep me (relatively) sane!

Last, but most importantly, thank you to all my fabulous readers.

It Takes Two

Chapter One

Alison Warner jabbed with her spoon at the dusting of chocolate powder on her third cappuccino until it no longer resembled a heart. Satisfied, she sank back against the red faux leather of the bench seat and yawned.

Her best friend, Simon sat opposite, talking animatedly, and Ali stared at the giant pink-purple stain that stood out like an open wound on the front of his crumpled white shirt, where she had accidentally spilled a large glass of red wine down it at her cousin Sasha's all-night engagement party. Her vigorous attempts to remove it had clearly made it worse.

Every so often, Simon leant forward, raised an arm in the air and gesticulated wildly with his agile hands, pressing his firm torso against the chrome trim of the white Formica table. It was most unlike him. Simon was usually the quiet one, letting Ali do most of the talking. But she was too tired to speak and was only half-listening.

She couldn't remember the last time she had stayed up all night and the previous two cups of coffee didn't seem to be doing a particularly good job of keeping her awake. The massive full-English breakfast – or 'All Day Special' as Josie Tate, the owner of the retro American diner, called it – that she and Simon had both just eaten, probably wasn't helping either. The coffees definitely hadn't done anything to relieve the pulse-like throbbing in her head. That had started shortly after Simon began talking about the number of people getting engaged lately. Marriage wasn't Ali's favourite subject, as Simon well knew, and as all those involved were either friends or family of hers, she hardly needed Simon to remind her. What she needed was at least eight hours' sleep, but that wasn't possible although it was Sunday and, strictly speaking, her day off.

'Everyone needs someone special in their life.' Simon stared into his coffee as if he expected *that someone* to suddenly appear in his cup. 'I've been thinking about it a lot lately. I mean, let's face it...' He shot a look at Ali. 'My dad was married with a kid, namely me, by the age of thirty. And dead from a heart attack at thirty-four. I'll be thirty-five in a couple of months.'

That caught Ali's attention. 'You're not suggesting you think there's a possibility you're going to die, are you? Because that's utter nonsense. You know your dad was born with a heart defect. Your heart's perfectly fine. It wasn't genetic.'

Simon waved his hand in the air. 'I know. I'm not talking about dying. Not yet, anyway. Although we all have to go sometime and no one knows when their time may be up. You're missing the point. I'm talking about the future. You know. Marriage. Kids. That sort of stuff.'

'B-o-ring.'

'You always say that. But we're not getting any younger, are we?'

Ali shrugged and let him carry on. She didn't have the energy to debate the subject. There were far more important things for her to think about. Like whether or not she would still have a job after her meeting later with her new boss, Aidan Rourke. Or the fact that, if the searing pain in her feet was anything to go by, there was a distinct possibility she might not be able to walk for several days.

She pressed her bare feet into the cool, black and white checked, ceramic tile floor of the Shimmering River Diner. It wasn't as refreshing as dangling her aching feet into the ice-cold waters of the Shimmering River itself, but she definitely didn't have the energy to do that. The tiles did at least reduce the burning in her soles. They also eased the pain of the seemingly identical, bulging blisters on each of her big toes and, with a sigh of relief, she closed her eyes for a few seconds to savour the sensation.

3

Birdsong, and the burbling waters of the Shimmering River competed with Simon's voice as a gentle breeze teased the leaves of the trees dotted along the riverbank, a few metres away. Even with her eyes shut, Ali could picture every inch of the view outside the window where she and Simon sat: the sun-bleached timber deck, stretching the full length of the diner; the wooden steps, slippery in the wet but now creaking like old, dry bones after the spell of excessively hot, June and July days and, the riverbank below, where the grass was a little too long and scattered with daisies, buttercups and other wild flowers. Here, this fork of the river was wide and shallow, lapping against ancient stepping stones which some people used to cross to the lush green fields opposite, ignoring the moss and lichen-covered stone bridge that provided a far safer route.

Less than a mile farther down, after meandering through the fields, the water tumbled over a two-metre-high drop into a lake and from there it met a deeper, fast-flowing fork. Together they formed a more substantial body of water and traced a wider, faster and in places, rapid-filled course down to the sea two miles beyond.

This stretch of the river, from the arch of the bridge, to the lake, the rapids and the wide mouth as the river spat itself into the sea, were all visible from the Shimmering River Diner, as was the village of Shimmering-on-Sea – which wasn't so much 'on sea', as 'above sea'.

The diner had the perfect vantage point, perched at the edge of one of two exceedingly steep hills overlooking the valley known as Shimmering Haven. The other hill rose up on the opposite side of the river, and the village, made up of three-hundred and fifty homes and a scattering of shops, stretched from the fields at the bottom to the cliff-like top. House prices in the village reflected the position of the house. The cheapest 'fishermen's cottage', prone to flooding at the river edge, to the wallet-busting 'sea-view mansion' on the crest of the hill. Not that any house in Shimmering-on-Sea could be classed as 'cheap' these days, not by most people's standards.

Ali loved the diner as much for its view as she did for its heavenly breakfasts. The lunches were pretty special too. And the afternoon teas and freshly baked scones, piled high with lashings of Josie's home-made strawberry jam, and thick fresh cream almost the colour of butter. Josie herself was a cheerful sight to behold, dressed as she always was, to emulate the quintessential American waitress, mixed with a few liberal helpings of Marilyn Monroe. For a woman closer to sixty than fifty, Josie Tate was wearing rather well.

Soon, Ali would have to leave the comfort of the cosy booth, put her high-heeled sandals back on and walk home … if she could. She needed to shower, get changed and head down to The Shimmering River and Water Sports Centre to meet her new boss. What a truly unappealing prospect that was.

Apart from the fact that the job of manager had been as good as promised to her by the recently retired former owner; the new guy didn't know a thing about running a water sports centre. From what Ali had heard, the only thing Aidan Rourke knew anything about was having fun – and spending his dad's vast fortune. A fortune acquired by Mr Rourke senior buying up small sports and leisure businesses, like the one where Ali had worked for the last four years, and turning them into high-end, exclusive clubs with sky-high membership fees. Or worse still, using the land on which they sat, to build ugly, executive homes – similar to the one in which Ali and her parents currently lived (although their house wasn't built by Rourke Homes, thankfully) – to be sold at extortionate prices.

Ali detested people like the Rourkes, who saw only pound signs where most people marvelled at the scenery, the sort who ruined villages and communities without a thought for those whose way of life the bulldozers and new-build estates were destroying. She hoped the Rourkes didn't have redevelopment plans for The Shimmering River and Water Sports Centre. It occupied a prime position set back slightly from the mouth of the river. A rickety old building made from wood and glass, it sat on tall, wood and iron stilts, built into the bank. Beside it sat a large, stone boathouse, a small dormitory building and a shower and toilet block together with a boat yard, a wooden pier and a concrete ramp leading down to the sea. In all, the centre covered several acres of land, and the entire village of Shimmering-on-Sea had talked of little else but the Rourkes' plans for the place, since news of their purchase of the centre had spread.

Ali disliked Aidan Rourke long before she'd been told he was taking what should have been her promotion. But she mustn't think about that. She'd have to find a way to get along with the entitled idiot, for everyone's sake, not just her own. And she would ask, point-blank what the plans were for the centre, unless he made it clear from the off.

Simon suddenly sounded as if his tie had become too tight. What had he been rabbiting on about? Glad to have her mind dragged away from unpleasant thoughts, Ali opened her eyes to see what was wrong. The tie wasn't the cause. It lay coiled on the table like a snake basking in the morning sun.

'So what do you say?' Simon looked somewhat sheepish. 'I expect the answer will be no, but I think it makes perfect sense.'

'What does?' She hadn't heard a word he had said for the last five minutes.

'Getting married. Us. You and me.' Simon swallowed and his Adam's apple jerked up and down his bronzed neck.

Ali blinked. At least three times. He was joking, of course.

Wasn't he?

Except he wasn't smiling and there wasn't the slightest hint of his trademark, playful, boyish grin.

Perhaps the copious amounts of alcohol they'd consumed at Sasha's all-night engagement party had completely addled his usually razor-sharp brain. Or maybe he needed more than the two cups of espresso coffee he'd already drunk and the third he was cradling in his palms, to bring him back to his senses. And yet … he wasn't even slurring his words.

'What?'

'Haven't you been listening?'

Ali shrugged. 'Kind of. But I'm tired. I think I must have missed something. What did you say? Exactly.'

'I said.' He took a deep breath and held it for a moment. 'Why don't we get married?'

Ali tried to look him in the eye as he breathed out, but his gaze darted around the baby-blue walls and the floor-to-ceiling windows of the diner, apparently following the agitated flight of a trapped bumble bee, buzzing like an alarm clock and repeatedly banging its head against the glass pane.

Perhaps she should do that to Simon.

'What?' Ali repeated. Now she sounded like the one being strangled.

'I think it's the answer to both our problems.' He cleared his throat, stood up, opened the top half of one of the windows a little wider and released the frantic bee which flew away without so much as a backward glance.

'I wasn't aware I had a problem.' Embarrassed and a little unsure of precisely what was happening, Ali sat upright and grabbed her spoon. Another jab removed the final trace of the former chocolate-powder heart.

Perhaps Simon had a point.

But his ludicrous suggestion definitely wasn't the way to resolve it. She let the spoon clatter into her saucer and, aware that he was staring at her with his mouth open, met his astonished look.

Simon shook his head as he resumed his seat. 'You're kidding, right?' His eyes were, as always, the clear cerulean blue of a summer sky, and now it was Ali who was having trouble looking at him.

'You're the one who's kidding.' She turned her head and stared out the window. She wasn't in the mood for this type of conversation at a little after seven o'clock on a Sunday morning. Not that she would ever be in the mood for a conversation about getting married. And absolutely *not* to *him*. What on earth was he thinking?

At least no one had heard him. They, and Josie Tate, were the only ones in the diner. It didn't officially open until nine on Sundays, but Josie had almost run them over as they tumbled out of the village hall where Sasha and her fiancé, John's party was still going strong, despite the licensing laws.

Josie had poked her head out of the car window. 'Are you OK? I nearly killed you!'

'Yep,' Ali replied, with a hic-cough, ignoring the fact that she was standing merely inches from the bonnet. Simon simply grinned and waved.

'Have you been there all night?' Josie nodded towards the hall. 'I left at midnight. There is no way I'd be able to do a day's work if I stayed up all night. My days of twenty-four-hour partying are sadly, history.'

'I have to go to work today.' Ali hic-coughed again. 'I'm meeting my new boss. I already know he's a git and it's going to be a disaster. I need coffee. And food.'

Josie smiled. 'Get in and I'll give you both a lift home.'

Ali hic-coughed three times as she and Simon clambered into the car. 'I don't suppose there's any chance of one of your super-duper breakfasts, is there?'

Josie shook her head, but in a manner that said yes, rather than no. 'I think I can rustle up a couple of my All-Day-Specials for the pair of you.'

Less than twenty minutes later, Ali and Simon tucked into crisp bacon, plump sausages, tasty mushrooms, perfectly fried tomatoes, toast and butter, and two poached eggs with gloriously runny, deep-yellow yolks. It was usually the perfect antidote to a night of heavy drinking. But not this morning, it seemed.

Ali returned her focus to Simon's face and he immediately looked down at his half-drunk espresso. She marvelled, as she always did, at the length of his dark lashes against his tanned cheekbones. She paid a small fortune for mascara that was supposed to make her lashes 'thick and luscious-looking' – whatever that meant – but they still fell short when compared to his. It was so annoying. He had lustrous hair, too. In the dappled glow of the early morning sunlight sneaking between the half-closed blinds, it was the colour of burnt caramel, with flecks of fudge. There was no denying that he was good-looking. Ali knew several women who 'fancied the pants off him'. But Ali didn't think of him in that way. She never had. They had been friends since the day she scrambled through a gap in her parents' garden fence and jumped, stark naked, into the paddling pool of their new neighbours, the Harts. Not that she remembered doing so; she was only two at the time, but that's the story Simon's mum, Maggie told to anyone who would listen. Much to Ali's embarrassment and in spite of the fact that it had happened more than thirty years ago, shortly before Simon's dad had his massive, fatal heart attack.

But in all that time, not once had either of them considered dating the other. Well, considered it maybe – and possibly more so after a few drinks –

but neither had actually acted on it, or so much as suggested it.

Until now. Out of the blue, after all those years and not even one, full-on kiss, the bloody idiot was asking her to marry him! OK, not asking, exactly. "Why don't we get married?" was more of a suggestion than a proposal, but it was a question that could completely change the dynamic of their life-long friendship.

Unless he hadn't meant that they should get married to one another. Perhaps he was simply saying that each of them should get married – to other people.

Well, if he wanted to jump into the fiery hell of matrimony that was his choice, but there was no way she would be joining him. Ever. And he should have known better than to make such a ridiculous statement, let alone phrase it as a question. It was enough to give a person palpitations.

'You can get married if you want, but count me out.' She stirred her coffee for the umpteenth time.

Shifting in his seat, his voice took on a firmer tone. 'It takes two, you know. I meant you and me. Why don't you and I cut through all this unsuccessful dating crap and simply get married to each other? We're best friends. We care about one another. It makes complete sense.'

The man had clearly lost his mind. It was the only explanation.

Ali glowered at him. 'It makes absolutely no sense at all. I'm amazed you'd even suggest such a ridiculous thing.' Coffee splashed over the rim of her cup as her spoon whipped through it. 'You must be mad. Unless you're kidding? You are, aren't you?'

Simon seemed coy and didn't reply, so for want of anything better to do and forgetting that the spoon was probably hot, Ali used it to slap the back of his hand as he cradled his coffee cup in its saucer.

'That hurt.' He frowned at her.

'Don't be a wimp.'

He licked his thumb and wiped at the red, oval mark on his hand and the remnants of cappuccino froth the spoon had deposited. 'Forget what I said. I'm already having second thoughts.'

'Don't scowl, Simon. It doesn't suit you. And please don't ever make a joke like that again. I might just take you seriously, and then where would we be?'

There was an odd glint in his eyes when he answered. 'Down the aisle and on our way to wedded bliss.' The faintest hint of a smile hovered on his lips.

'Up the creek without a paddle, more like. You utter dingbat.' She slapped his forearm and grinned, leaning back and relaxing once again now that the awkward moment was over. He must have realised she had been thinking about her new boss and had used the marriage thing to take her mind off it.

Simon ran a hand through his hair and looked out the window. 'Speaking of paddles, doesn't your new boss arrive today?'

'Oh yeah. I'd completely forgotten it was today,' Ali lied. She grinned at him but his attention seemed fixed on a tractor ploughing one of the fields in the distance. She pushed herself upright again and glanced at her watch. 'Look at the time. It's almost seven-fifteen. I've got to get home, grab a few minutes' sleep if possible, then have a shower and make myself look fabulously professional before the privileged git shows his face and waves his silver spoon in the air.' She blew on her coffee and gulped it down as fast as the heat of it would allow.

Simon gave her a soulful look. 'You see. That's why you should marry me. I know what's on your calendar better than you do.'

Ali tutted. 'Will you please stop using such foul language, Simon Hart. Even jokingly. And especially on a Sunday. You know I can't bear the M-word on a good day, and today is definitely not going to be one of those. Why did you let me drink so much last night? And dance until I couldn't walk, knowing that I had to meet my new boss this morning? Some bloody husband you'd be.'

'Marry me, and you'll see what sort of husband I'd be. I think you'd be surprised.'

Ali frowned and, trying to ignore the pain in her feet, stood to gather her belongings. 'I know you too well to be surprised – although I am surprised that you're still going on about it. A joke's a joke, Simon. Don't beat it to death. I mean it.' She reached across the padded bench seat to grab her handbag. 'Stop talking about marriage. You know how I feel about it.' She bent down to retrieve her strappy sandals from where she had slipped them off, but they were too far to reach. 'I am never, ever, ever, going to marry anyone. Not in this lifetime. Not if my life depended on it. Not if someone paid me a million, billion, trillion pounds to tie the knot.' She stretched her back. 'I can't reach my shoes. Will you get them for me, please? They're by your feet.'

Simon sighed, bent down and picked up the sandals by the straps, dangling them towards Ali on his fingers. 'Your shoes, m'lady.'

'Thank you, kind sir.'

She slid her feet between the straps, which felt more like razor wire than pale blue leather and the aches and pains of too many hours dancing on very high heels really came home to roost.

'What's wrong?'

'These shoes weren't made for dancing.'

'Those shoes weren't made for walking, either. Why do you insist on inflicting so much pain on yourself?'

'Looking sensational comes at a very high price, but we women are made of strong stuff. And they're absolutely gorgeous. Even you have to admit that.'

'They're sandals, Ali. OK, they're a pretty colour, but the nails in my garden fence aren't anywhere near as sharp and pointed as the heels on those things.'

'Heathen. I have it on good authority that shoes are an art form. How could I possibly consider spending my life with a man who doesn't understand that?'

'There are far more important things in life than shoes – and far better reasons to spend your life with me than whether or not I like them.'

Ali slapped her hand against her chest. 'Nothing is more important than shoes – according to my mother. Except money. And you don't have very much of that, either.'

Something flickered across Simon's eyes. He opened his mouth to reply, but obviously thought better of it and merely shrugged.

Ali grinned at him. 'If I were ever crazy enough to consider it – which I'm not and never shall be – I suppose, on reflection, it might as well be with you. You're the best friend any girl could have. You're not bad looking and you've got a reasonably well-paid job. Although I firmly believe you should be headmaster of that crappy school and not just head of the Shimmering-on-Sea River School, Maths department which, unless I'm sadly out of date, consists of you, you and you.'

'Gosh, thanks. I think. But you're forgetting my assistant, Miss Quinn, so that makes two of us in the Maths department. Although technically, Jane is the school admin secretary, so she assists every teacher there, but I like to think she's mine, all mine. And, I firmly believe you should've got the job of manager of The Shimmering River and Water Sports Centre, instead of the position being given to the owner's son. But as we've discovered this morning, we don't always get what we want. Anyway, there's clearly no way you're going to be able to hobble home in those things. I'll call a cab and drop you off on the way to mine.'

'Call a cab? It's Sunday, Simon. They charge a fortune on Sundays. Especially at seven-fifteen-ish in the morning. Don't waste your money. I would suggest we call my mum, but we both know that would be like unleashing a wild tiger at this time on a Sunday. And Dad will be out on his now obligatory, three-hour, Sunday morning run. So the only option really is for you to carry me. It's only a mile and that's what friends are for.' She threw him a cheeky smile and a wink.

Simon arched his brows. 'Now you're definitely the one's who's kidding. Carry you? After being up all night and dancing for most of it I can hardly carry myself. And after that breakfast you've just eaten and the three coffees you drank, there's no way I'm carrying you. Plus, you seem to be ignoring the fact that it's a mile as the crow flies. On the ground, it's more like three. Most of it, uphill.'

'Humph! And you think you'd make a good husband? You're clearly deluded, Mr Hart.' Ali removed the vice-like sandals and sighed. 'But OK. Calling a cab isn't such a bad idea given the circumstances, I suppose. Not as chivalrous, but a very close second. I take it back. You may make someone a good husband one day. But it definitely won't be me. And it's just as well you were joking. If I turn out anything like my mum, you'd hate me.'

'I'll never hate you, Ali.' Simon dialled the number for a cab as he grinned at her. 'And your mum's not that bad. In spite of her views on shoes … and money. She's going through a rough time. Separation and divorce are never easy and it's probably twice as difficult for two divorce lawyers. They know exactly what to expect.'

'They know exactly how to bring out the worst in one another. Living with them is increasingly becoming like living in a war zone.'

'I've already told you the answer to that problem. To all our problems.'

'Oh for heaven's sake, shut up!'

He ignored the face she pulled and spoke to the cab company instead.

'They'll be here in five minutes,' he said, shoving his phone back in his trouser pocket. He took her arm and linked it through his.

'Will you at least give me a piggyback to the door, please? My feet are absolutely killing me. I hope this new boss of mine lets me sit down to tell him everything he needs to know because there is no way on this planet that I can stand and talk to him. And showing him around the place is completely out of the question.'

'That should get your working relationship off to an exceptionally good start. Here.' Simon turned his back to her. 'Jump on.'

She clambered onto the padded seat and from there, onto Simon's back. He wrapped his arms around her legs and she clung to his shoulders. 'Giddy up,' she said. 'And d'you know what? I think I'd better go directly to the centre. I can shower there and I always keep some spare clothes in my office. If I go home, I'll have to face Mum and Dad at some stage this morning, and I'm definitely not in the mood to be caught in the middle of one of their ongoing arguments today. Plus, I don't think I'd make it home and back, seeing as how I'm virtually crippled.'

'And whose fault is that?' He marched towards the door as if Ali weighed no more than one of his Maths books.

'Yours, of course. You should've stopped me dancing.'

'As if you'd have listened to me.'

'I might've.' She rested her head against his shoulder. 'I do love you, you know Simon. Oh! But not—'

'But not enough to marry me. I know. I think we've established that.'

'Well, you were joking anyway.'

'Yeah. I was joking, Ali. You're absolutely right. You, me and marriage. That's an equation that would never add up.'

Chapter Two

How ten tiny men with massive sledge hammers had got inside Simon's skull, he had no idea, but as his head was pounding and, he was sure, cracking from the inside out, they obviously had. Or something very similar. And clearly his understanding of the phrase: 'fast acting' was immeasurably different to that of the manufacturers of headache tablets. He had taken two of the puny-looking pills before he'd collapsed on top of his bed this morning, but more than an hour later, when his mum knocked on his bedroom door, it sounded as if she was using a battering ram instead of her hand, and a foghorn to announce that she was: 'bringing a refreshing cup of tea'.

Just as well he hadn't brought a woman home from John and Sasha's engagement party. Although, feeling as he did, he would have had to tell the woman – as he just had to tell his mum – to 'Please get the hell out and let me sleep.' Not that his mum had taken any notice. Neither would she have done so if there had been a woman in his bed. She would simply have brought an extra cup of tea, sat herself on the edge of the bed, asked if they'd both had a good night and whether they'd like anything for breakfast. As she was doing now, to him. He really must have another word with her about his privacy.

She meant well, of course, and she had a heart of gold, but he was thirty-five years old, for Christ's sake, and was perfectly capable of making his own tea. Although possibly not this morning. But more to the point, the reason he had paid for the house to be converted into two flats was so that he and his mum could lead completely separate lives but still spend time together without having to travel further than a flight of stairs and a dividing hallway. It was his own fault. He should not have given her a key to his flat.

The problem was, she had never really recovered from the shock of his dad's early death. Samuel Hart had been the love of her life and when he died, she devoted all her time to Simon in a futile attempt to get over her loss. Thankfully, she wasn't the clingy type, but she was very caring. Overly so. She was happy to let Simon live his own life, go to university, go travelling if he wanted to, provided he kept in touch, but when he was at home, it seemed she wanted to spend as much time with him as possible, and thought doors were only shut to keep out draughts, not to keep out prying mothers. He hoped that having separate flats would set up some kind of barrier. At least one where she felt she had to knock and wait to be invited in; not simply tap on the door and enter. It hadn't worked like that, unfortunately.

When the conversion work was complete and he had given her a key to his flat he had tried to set up some ground rules.

'This is for emergencies only. When I'm here you can knock on the door and I'll let you in and I'll do the same with you.'

'There's no need for that, sweetheart,' Maggie had said. 'Why would we need to lock the doors to our individual flats? We can simply make sure the main front door is locked.'

'Er, no, Mum. We both need some privacy. I think it's best if we lock our own doors.'

'Why would we need privacy? Obviously I wouldn't barge into your bedroom or the bathroom without knocking, but we've shared a lounge and kitchen for years. I can see why you want your own living space. You're a grown man and I respect that, but locking doors is a bit unnecessary, isn't it? We've never locked doors before.'

'We've never had a door to lock, other than the front door. But now we do. And we should use them. I mean, what if I brought a woman home? I wouldn't want you popping in if I was … otherwise engaged, let's say. You might find it a bit … embarrassing.'

It was somewhat disconcerting that she had laughed at that. 'Bring a woman home? You say that as if it's something new. You're always bringing Ali home and neither of you have minded me popping in when she's here.'

There wasn't much he could say to disagree with that. 'But Ali's just a friend. What I meant was, I might bring a woman home who was … more than a friend to me.'

Maggie smiled and raised her brows. 'Oh. To have sex, you mean. Well, why didn't you simply come right out and say it? I wouldn't find it at all embarrassing. I'd be pleased. If you were actually having sex with a woman it might mean you liked her enough to take things further, and that might lead to marriage and babies. I'd love to be a granny. You wouldn't have to pay for outside help or hire a nanny or anything. I'd be on hand to look after the kids whenever you wanted, day or night.'

Quite how the subject had gone so rapidly from bringing home a woman for sex to bringing home a wife and kids, was beyond his comprehension.

'Yes. Thanks for that. Don't start planning your babysitting schedule just yet. It may take me some time to find a woman I like enough to spend the rest of my life with.'

'You like Ali. I've always thought the two of you would make a perfect couple. If only she could set aside her rather odd views on matrimony. I blame her parents for that. Ali could quote the divorce statistics for the year before she could do her times tables. Don't get me wrong. Tabitha and Tom are lovely people, but the conversation in their house somehow always seems to turn to divorce. I know that's what they do for a living, but still. It doesn't seem right to me. And if what I hear is true, it seems they may be heading in that direction themselves. Such a shame. When we lived next door to them, they seemed so much in love. Just like your dad and I. But let's not dwell on that. What Ali needs is to move out of that house and start a family of her own.'

Perhaps that was when the seed of an idea – clearly an incredibly stupid idea – had formed in Simon's head. Or maybe he was simply getting tired of comparing every woman he met to Ali and have the woman fall short. But marriage to Ali? Was that even possible?

At least he'd now got the answer to that. A big fat *no*! And the stupid thing was, he wasn't even sure he wanted to marry Ali in the first place. But at John and Sasha's engagement party, John had slapped him on the back.

'Do you realise you're the only one of our friends from school, who isn't married or engaged? Apart from Ali, that is. But I meant you're the last man standing, mate. Hold out for as long as you can. Some lucky woman will set her sights on you and before you know it, you'll be having an engagement party just like this one.'

'Lucky me.' Simon was certain there would never be another engagement party like Sasha and John's. Once word got out of the all-nighter, the Local Authority would possibly keep a much closer eye on who hired out the village hall, and probably have someone come and lock up at an appropriate time, no doubt.

But John's words, coming so soon after his own mum talking about marriage and Ali in the same sentence had got him thinking. And wondering. And drinking far too much for his own good. Like the idiot he knew only too well he could sometimes be, he'd only gone and asked her. At least she hadn't laughed in his face. Well, not right away. But she had made it abundantly clear that there was more chance of him leading a school trip to Mars than there was of being her husband.

Ali's husband? Did he really want that? They'd been best mates for years and never once had he thought about kissing her, let alone having sex with her. How would that even work? He'd never felt the urge and yet they'd been in some pretty close situations.

That wasn't completely true. He had felt the urge. More than once, if he was going to be honest with himself. When she smiled at him in the way she did, or shoved her long blonde hair away from her incredibly pretty face. Or when she lost her temper with him and pursed her luscious-looking lips. Or when her blue eyes changed to an almost iridescent aqua. Or when she laughed. Or when she touched him. Or … Oh shit. Why didn't he simply face the fact. He wanted to grab her and pull her into his arms at least once every single day for the last few years. But something always stopped him.

She hated the idea of marriage. None of her relationships lasted more than a year. Some, far less. The second she thought things were getting a little too serious, she ran for the hills. Figuratively speaking. He loved her. He loved being with her. He couldn't risk doing anything to ruin that. He couldn't face the thought of losing her.

But this morning, he'd nearly done exactly that. What had he been thinking? It was all these sodding engagements. They were getting to him. That was the only answer. They were getting to Ali too. As was her parents' impending separation and divorce. If anything, Ali was even more anti-marriage now than she had ever been. And that was really some going.

'Simon? Are you all right?' his mum was saying.

He met the anxious look in her eyes. 'No, Mum, I'm not. And you sitting on my bed nursing that cup of tea isn't helping. Can't you please take on board that this is *my* flat? That I had this place converted into flats for a reason. I need some sodding privacy. Not you bursting in whenever you feel like it. Can't you knock and wait for me to say whether or not you can come in, at the very least? I knew I shouldn't have bought this bloody house from you. What I should have done was bought a place of my own away from here.'

'But I did knock, sweetheart. You didn't answer. I knew you'd been out all night so I thought you might like a cup of tea, and....' Her voice trailed off and the cheerful smile was gradually replaced with a grimace. 'Oh, I see. Are you saying that you only did all this because you felt you had to? That you'd have preferred to live far away from me? I … I didn't realise you felt like that. I … I thought you liked being with me. But of course, that was silly of me. You're a young man with a life of your own and—'

'Stop right there,' he interrupted. He hadn't meant to hurt her. Christ, what was wrong with him today? First he proposes to Ali. Now he breaks his mum's heart. 'I'm sorry, Mum. I didn't mean that. And I didn't mean to snap at you.'

'That's all right,' she sniffed. 'I understand. I'm just a silly old woman suffocating her lovely son.'

She went to stand but he gently put his hand on her arm to stop her. He took the teacup from her shaking hand and placed it on the bedside table. He then took both her hands in his and squeezed them tight – but not too tight. She suddenly looked very fragile … and old.

'I love you, Mum. With all my heart. I love living close to you. You're not a silly old woman and you're not suffocating me. But yes, I am a grown man and I do want some privacy. You should, too. You're only sixty-three. You still have a lifetime ahead of you. Don't you want to meet someone special? Don't you want a life of your own that doesn't revolve around me? I bought the house from you so that you'd have money. So that you could do all the things you should've been doing – would've been doing if Dad were alive. Plus, I bought it so that we could still be close. The hesitation I had wasn't for me. It was that you might still do exactly what you are doing.'

'Interfering. Ruining your life.' She wouldn't meet his eyes.

'Putting me and my needs before yourself. Putting your life on hold until I find someone who you think may replace you. Sacrificing your needs for mine.'

She raised tearful eyes to his. 'It's a mother's job to take care of her children. It's not a sacrifice. You're my world, sweetheart.'

He shifted his position so that he could wrap his arms around her. 'And you're mine, Mum. But that doesn't mean we can't share that world with other people. You want me to be happy, I know that. Well, I want you to be happy, too. And I need to do things for myself. Make my own tea, my own breakfast. Do my own washing. That's why I wanted us to live separately. I want a mum I can chat and laugh with, as we do, but not a cook, cleaner and general dogsbody. I want you to come for coffee, or lunch or dinner, or just to tell me about your day. I don't want that day to revolve around me. I'm not sure I'm explaining this properly.'

Maggie raised her hand and gently brushed his cheek. 'You're explaining it perfectly, sweetheart.

And I love you even more, if that's possible – which of course, it isn't.'

'I really am sorry I snapped.'

'Forget it, sweetheart. What you need is sleep, I expect. Not me sitting on your bed. I'll leave you in peace.' She got to her feet and smiled. 'And next time I'll knock and wait to be invited in.'

'Actually, Mum. What I need is a cup of coffee. And a chat. If you have time, that is.'

She beamed at him. 'I think I have a free half hour. Your place or mine?'

Simon grinned. 'Mine. It's closer.'

'Well, you'd better get up then. That coffee won't make itself, sweetheart.' She winked and left the room.

'I think I may regret what I said,' he called after her, laughing as he jumped out of bed, his headache gone completely. It seemed that his already pretty wonderful relationship with his mum had actually taken an even better turn this morning. It was a pity he couldn't say the same about his relationship with Ali. But perhaps his mum would have a few ideas on what he should do about that.

Chapter Three

The manager's job should have been Ali's. Everyone said as much. Even her own parents – and they didn't want her working at The Shimmering River and Water Sports Centre in the first place. A complete waste of a good – and exceedingly expensive – education, as far as Tabitha and Tom Warner were concerned. Not that the cost of her education was money well spent in any event, in Ali's opinion. Unfortunately, she took after her grandmother, Gertie, not her mum, in the brains department – quick-witted, but not overly intelligent. Good with her hands, not her mind. Preferred swimming in the sea to burying her head in study books. And she didn't take any notice of her parents' opinions on her career choice. She would far rather work at the centre than be stuck in an office all day, as they were. Albeit in exceptionally grand offices in London, with state-of-the-art air conditioning and interior design budgets large enough to make a person's eyes water. Ali would suffocate in such an environment. She would wither away and die like a delicate flower.

Not that Ali was either delicate or flower-like. She had the constitution of an ox, so Gertie was always telling her. Gertie also told her she was as stubborn as a mule. And as flighty as a magpie. Gertie liked similes. She sprinkled them into her conversations as liberally as she sprinkled sugar in her tea. It didn't matter to her if half of them made no sense at all. She recently described her own daughter, Tabitha, Ali's mum, as being as cool as a cucumber and as dizzy as a cat on a hot tin roof, all in the same sentence.

'Aren't they the complete opposite of each other?' Ali had asked.

Gertie gave her trademark throaty chuckle, caused, her doctor had told her, from smoking too many cigarettes in her past. 'No, Ali-ba-ba,' Gertie said, using her pet name for her grand-daughter. 'Your mum's like a whirling dervish at the moment. Keeps switching from one mood to another. One minute we're all basking in the sunshine of her smile, the next we're in the middle of an ice storm. I think your mum and dad need their heads bashed together. That'd soon sort out this divorce nonsense.'

Ali had changed the subject. Her parents' upcoming divorce was another conversation she didn't want to have.

Now, instead of being manager, she was waiting to meet her jumped-up new boss and she wasn't looking forward to it. Still a little hung-over from last night, something else was niggling at her – apart from Aidan Rourke's impending arrival. Simon had obviously been joking this morning but it had slightly unnerved her. They'd been such good, close friends for so many years. Why now? Why would he suddenly make a joke about them getting married?

'There is no smoke without fire,' Gertie would have said. Was Simon, in an obtusely roundabout way, trying to tell Ali that he wanted more from her than friendship? That his feelings had suddenly changed and his love had gone from platonic to passionate?

There was nothing passionate about the way he suggested they should get married. Nothing even remotely romantic either. It seemed he merely thought it might be a way of solving the problems he believed they had. Hers – that she had a complete aversion to marriage and his – that he lived under his mother's thumb.

OK, not under her thumb, exactly. If anything, Maggie Hart lived under his. She was so devoted to him, she had no real life of her own. She dreaded the thought of losing him; so much so that she'd somehow managed to find the money to have her house converted into flats, just so that he would live nearby. At the time, Ali had asked Simon whether Maggie had obtained a mortgage to pay for the work, or whether she had savings, or perhaps, money left over from the life insurance on his dad, but Simon had been so vague about it and clearly didn't want to discuss it, so she'd let the matter drop. She must ask him about it again at some stage. Not that it was any of her business. But it was so unlike him. Simon usually told her everything – and she, him. They had no secrets from each other as far as she was aware. Not one. Or so she thought until today. Was he keeping his true feelings for her a secret?

He had been behaving out of character lately. She hadn't thought much about it before, what with her parents' marriage suddenly falling apart and then her boss selling up – and to the Rourkes, of all people. They were well-known in the surroundings counties, not only for their wealth but also their complete indifference to anyone other than themselves. Since hearing that the centre was their latest acquisition, Simon's erratic behaviour had almost completely passed her by. The more she thought about it, the more she realised something had definitely changed.

'Penny for them.'

'What?' Ali's head shot up at the sound of the stranger's deep voice. Her mouth fell open at the sight of the stranger's face and her body suddenly woke up from its deeply hung-over state of lethargy to a state of excited frenzy. Holy Hell, this man was hot. Hotter than hot. Had her body actually caught fire just by looking at him? Heat flooded her cheeks and if she opened her mouth again to speak, she would no doubt see steam come out instead of words.

He smiled, and whistles blew in her head. He walked towards her, and alarm bells clanged fifty to the dozen. Who was this man? What was happening to her? Was this what people meant by love at first sight? It was definitely lust at first sight. She wanted to rip her clothes off and throw herself on the desk in front of him.

Her clothes! Damn it, damn it, damn it. Why hadn't she gone home to change? Why hadn't she worn a dress, at least? Why had she grabbed her tracksuit, tied her hair into a ponytail and removed all traces of make-up from last night? Why had she slipped on her flip-flops instead of the eye-poppingly expensive, designer trainers her mum had bought her 'as a little gift' the other day; the ones she'd carefully replaced in the gold tissue paper and designer box they'd come in and safely placed in the bottom draw of her desk because designer trainers and water sports didn't mix as far as she was concerned.

'Please don't get up.' The man had an excited look in his eye as he reached her desk. As if he had found a pot of gold, not a scruffy young woman.

This definitely couldn't be her new boss. He couldn't be.

Finally, she found her voice. 'Sorry. All-night party. Bit hung-over. Who are you?' Great. She sounded like a moron. That went nicely with the overall look of layabout she must have given, seated as she was with her feet up on a half-open drawer, leaning back in her battered swivel chair, a half-drunk cup of coffee in one hand, a bar of chocolate from the vending machine, in the other.

He raised dark, perfectly shaped brows. 'I'm Aidan. Aidan Rourke. And you, I assume, must be Alison Warner.'

All the bubbles burst at once. This man. This demi-god. This sex machine. This gorgeous hunk of athletic-looking manhood, *was* Aidan Rourke. The git? No! It couldn't be. The universe was having a laugh. So much for looking professional when she met him. Her hangover had definitely put paid to that intention.

She nodded. What else could she do? She couldn't speak. She wanted to cry like a baby. In her thirty-three years on this earth, she had never fallen deeply, madly, passionately in love with anyone. In the last five seconds there was a distinct possibility that she had done all three – four if you counted 'hungrily'. She could eat this man up right here, right now. She wanted to lick and nibble every last inch of him. Every. Last. Inch. And he was the one person on the planet she could absolutely *not* feel this way about. Absolutely. Not.

She was in trouble. Up to her eyes in it. She couldn't fall for a privileged, arrogant, inconsiderate bastard like Aidan Rourke. She couldn't.

'You seem somewhat apprehensive,' he said, every syllable bringing a new goosebump to her skin. 'I completely understand that. I hope I can set your mind at ease.'

He perched casually on the far edge of her desk and smiled, which had completely the opposite effect to making her feel at ease. He appeared to be waiting for her to respond but she didn't.

'OK. Let me explain.' He leant forward. 'The position of manager should've been yours, Alison.'

'Ali,' she squeaked.

'Ali. I like that. Well Ali, let's get this sorted right away, OK? It is. I'm promoting you to manager with effect from today. I'm also giving you a pay rise to match your position. The only thing I know about water sports is enjoying them. I don't know what goes on behind the scenes and I have no desire to. That's your job. You keep this place running – or should that be, flowing, smoothly and I'll keep out of your hair. Deal?'

What had just happened? 'What?'

'Don't you want the job? I thought you'd be happy. Is there a problem? Or is there something else you want?'

You, she wanted to say. Instead she coughed, pulled herself upright and forced a smile. 'Are you serious?' Thank heavens the squeaky voice had gone. She sounded more like her usual self at last.

He leant closer and she almost reached out and grabbed him. 'Deadly,' he whispered.

She didn't doubt that for a minute.

'You're making me the manager? From today?'

'Uh-huh.'

He even made "uh-huh" sound sexy. This man was dynamite.

She coughed again. 'Why?'

He furrowed his brows and his dark, molasses-coloured eyes seemed to seep into hers. She had to pull herself together. His laughter was like a heavenly chorus. She was really losing the plot.

'Haven't I made that clear? I don't like work. Complete allergy to it. Fun, yes. Work, no. So here's the deal. You work, I play.' He laughed some more. 'Of course, I will have to pop in from time to time. Dad's a bit of a tyrant and he'll expect that. And, now that I've seen some of the … delights the place has to offer, I think I'll definitely be popping in more frequently than I'd originally planned. But as to the day-to-day running of the place, that's now down to you. We may need to make a few changes but there's no need to discuss those now.'

He brushed a wayward strand of hair from Ali's face, and in doing so, took the words she was about to say and made them disappear.

'You weren't the only one who was apprehensive about today, Ali,' he continued. 'But I think you and I are going to get along just fine. Better than fine, in fact. A lot, lot better. Don't you agree?'

She nodded.

'Excellent. I can see you've got a lot on your mind and I believe that today is actually your day off, so I won't detain you.' He slid from the desk and smiled the sexiest smile she'd ever seen. 'It was lovely to meet you, Ali and I'm already looking forward to the next time. Enjoy your day. See you soon. Very, very soon.'

He was gone as quickly and as quietly as he had arrived, but something – other than just the promotion – had changed in Ali's life. Was it for better, or for worse? And why had damn marriage vows suddenly pop into her head? She must be more hung-over than she had thought. That was the only explanation.

Wasn't it?

Chapter Four

Ali limped into Oakwood Crescent and immediately stopped in her tracks. All she wanted was a peaceful afternoon dozing in front of the TV with a bottle of red wine and a pizza with all the toppings, followed sometime later by a luxurious bath and an early night. But a relaxing time probably wasn't on the cards. The sprawling, new-build house she shared with her parents, sat dead-centre of the Crescent's raised curve, ensuring it could been seen from either end of the street. It gave the impression of 'Lording it' over each of the three houses either side – which was one of the reasons her mum had chosen it, and from where Ali stood, she could see both her parents' cars were parked on the brick-paved driveway.

She reluctantly hobbled onward, her flip-flops slapping both the pavement and her soles. For the past few weeks her parents had arranged things so that only one of them was home at any given time. She was becoming more anxious with every step.

Either they'd got their timings mixed up, or one of them was out and hadn't taken their car, which seemed unlikely. Other than her dad's three-hour Sunday run, her parents went virtually everywhere in their respective cars, the few exceptions being, the train to London each day for work – and even then they each drove separately to the local station two miles inland – or if they popped down to the village shops for something.

Raised voices greeted her the moment she stepped onto the sloping drive.

After the confusing and rather disturbing day she'd had, the last thing she needed was to listen to her parents arguing. Perhaps if she told them about her sudden promotion and pay increase, they might stop throwing insults at one another and shower some goodwill and happiness on her. They were, after all, often telling her she lacked drive and ambition, so the promotion should please them both. They had never understood why she had taken the job at the centre in the first place. They assumed their only daughter would follow in their footsteps. How wrong they had been about that. Ali had seen how their careers had affected them. She had no intention of travelling down a similar path. Fitness and the outdoors, especially anything to do with water, were her true love. And she was as stubborn and determined as her parents when it came to getting what she wanted, provided it was something she wanted badly enough.

She wasn't going to get what she wanted this afternoon. Nearing the front door, the shouting grew louder. Should she simply turn around and leave her parents to it?

She could go to see her other best friend, Jules, or pop around the corner to Sasha's. But since Jules had started planning her own wedding, she was turning into a bit of a Bridezilla, and newly-engaged Sasha would no doubt be going down the same path. Sasha would probably be cuddling up with John, anyway. Jules' fiancé, Bruce would be playing golf, as he usually did on a Sunday, come hell or high water … or hangover. All of them would be nursing one of *those* judging by the amount of alcohol they all consumed last night.

There was always Simon. She could go to his. Or maybe not. Now that she was questioning his feelings, would it be too soon to crash out on his bed as she had so many times before, without there now being a sense of awkwardness?

Besides, she didn't really want company. What she wanted was the TV to herself, and some peace and quiet so that she could think. She definitely needed to think about the day she'd had. Think about Simon. About her promotion. But mostly about the weird feelings she'd experienced when she'd met the unbelievably gorgeous, Aidan Rourke.

If only she could talk to her mum about it. But that would be a complete waste of time. And a very short conversation. Tabitha Warner would only be interested in hearing two things about Aidan. Was he single? Was he wealthy? Nothing else mattered in her opinion these days. Not feelings. Not love. Not companionship, or compatibility. If the man was single and wealthy, marry him. If it didn't work out, get a good lawyer – like her – and take the jerk to the cleaners. A very odd attitude for a woman who had herself married for love and whose marriage had lasted for nearly thirty-six years. Until a few short months ago.

Being the daughter of two successful divorce lawyers definitely had its perks, financially, but the dinner conversation usually revolved round failure. Failed marriages to be precise. From a very young age, Ali had been able to quote the statistics of how many marriages ended in divorce and it was one of the reasons she decided she never wanted to add to the numbers. Admittedly, the divorce rate had apparently decreased slightly over the last few years, no doubt due to the fact that more people lived together now without actually marrying, but the numbers were still high. She could say with some certainty that those who married younger were more likely to divorce, as were women over fifty-five – the age group into which her mum fell, having recently turned fifty-nine. Every day, Ali had heard how couples, who were once so much in love, were suddenly at each other's throats. Either it was a cruel twist of fate, or people made bad choices where love was concerned. And they argued over the most ridiculous things. Like who would get the vase that someone or other had bought them – a vase both had agreed was hideous until the contemplated divorce. Suddenly, neither party could live without that vase. Or something they had both loved because of sentimental reasons, they now both despised simply because it had once meant so much. It was getting that way with her parents.

Ali took a deep breath and opened the front door of the Warner family home. Not that the eight bedroomed, architect designed house would be the family home for much longer. Tom and Tabitha Warner were going their separate ways and it was becoming more apparent with each passing day that it was going to be an acrimonious divorce. A divorce in which Ali was stuck firmly in the middle.

Her parents were standing in the hall and they turned towards her like bulls about to charge.

'Ali! Tell your father it's completely out of the question. He knows I'm having friends round for dinner on Friday, so removing the dining table and chairs to his den of iniquity on Thursday simply won't do.' Tabitha flicked a lock of long blonde hair over her shoulder and crossed her arms in front of her ample chest.

'Remind your mother that the dining table and chairs belong to me and I shall remove them whenever and to wherever I see fit. Also point out that my new house is not and never shall be a den of iniquity. I am not having sex with someone else, but if I were, it would be as part of a loving, happy and perfectly healthy relationship. Not that your mother can remember what sex is, of course.'

'Assure your father that I remember sex quite clearly. Even though two seconds and a gasp is hardly memorable.'

'Enough!' Ali shoved the front door shut with her elbow and threw her keys into the hand-carved wooden bowl on the hall table.

The bowl was teak and came from Thailand where the newly-wed Mr and Mrs Warner had purchased it on their honeymoon nearly thirty-six years ago. It had been in the hall of each of the three houses the Warners had owned and was always displayed on a hall table similar to the ebony one on which it now sat. No doubt they would be arguing over that bowl before too long.

Tabitha gave Ali a startled look. 'There's no need to shout, darling. Or slam doors.'

'No,' said Tom. 'Your mother already has that down to a fine art.'

'Stop it, both of you. I've had a really tiring day after no sleep at all last night. I could do with not getting dragged into one of your ongoing arguments the minute I open the front door.'

'Well honestly, darling. How am I supposed to know what sort of day you've had? And staying up all night was your choice entirely. I came home at a sensible hour. God alone knows what time your father skulked away. No doubt with some bimbo or other on his arm.'

'I left shortly after you, and alone, as you damn well know. You tried to run me over in the car park.'

'I did no such thing. I didn't see you.'

'Oh, you saw me.'

'Stop it! Why is everything always about the two of you these days? Instead of acting like spoilt children you could start behaving like civilised adults and sort this out between yourselves. Please leave me out of it. I love you both and I hate this squabbling.'

'Tell your father that. He's the one who started the argument.'

'I did no such thing. I simply told your mother when the removal company were coming to take my belongings.'

'The day before my dinner party. A dinner party that's been written on the calendar for weeks.'

'How am I supposed to know what's written on the calendar? It's your calendar. You told me so in no uncertain terms. You also told me not to check what you were getting up to, remember? Not that I was. I'm not in the least bit interested in what you do.'

Ali let out an ear-piercing scream and both Tabitha and Tom unwittingly took a few steps back.

'Alison?' Tom frowned at her. 'Why on earth did you make that dreadful noise?'

'Because I've had it, OK? You were in love once. Can't you remember that?' She grabbed the heart-shaped wooden bowl, the keys jangling against the sides like chains. 'Remember this? You always told me that the reason you keep this by the front door is so that, no matter how stressful your day may have been, the first thing you see when you come home is this bowl, and it takes you straight back to your honeymoon and idyllic walks along the beach, hand in hand. What's going to happen to this?'

Tabitha and Tom briefly exchanged glances.

'You can have that,' Tom said. 'Even though I paid for it.' He turned away and strode off towards his study.

'I don't want the bloody thing,' Tabitha shrieked. 'I've always hated it. I only pretended to like it because you bought it the day we arrived and I didn't want to hurt your feelings.'

He glowered at her over his shoulder. 'You were always good at pretence. But it's been a long time since you cared about anyone's feelings other than your own.' He slammed the door behind him.

'You wouldn't know a feeling if it jumped up and bit you on that Pinocchio-like nose of yours! Ignorant pig,' Tabitha snarled, slamming the dining room door behind her.

Ali tossed the bowl onto the table sending keys sliding over the edge and onto the black, polished table top. Neither of them wanted the bowl, it seemed. And yet they still managed to argue over it. She reached out to return the keys but her mobile rang and instead she answered that.

'Welcome to the Warner family home. A haven of happiness, tranquillity and love.'

'You what, babe?' Jules, her other best friend asked, after a momentary silence.

'Nothing. Just came home to Mum and Dad arguing again.'

'No change there then.'

'Nope. How was your day? Mine's been weird. Please tell me something to cheer me up.'

'We're going to The Golden Dragon. Want to join us?'

'We, who?'

'Me and Sasha. John's going to come along later. And Simon might, I think. My darling fiancé, will be stuck at the nineteenth hole on the Shimmering River Golf Course for some time, I expect, but even he may show his ugly mug at some point. He's paying though, although he doesn't know that yet.'

Ali glanced towards the vacant sitting room; the vision of her crashed out in front of the TV briefly appearing before her, but her gaze drifted to the closed doors of the dining room and her dad's study and the vision was gone in a flash.

'I'm on the way. Oh, but actually I can't walk. I've just hobbled back from the centre and I can't move another step. My feet are killing me. I'll have to call a cab. And I suppose I should get changed. I'm in my tracksuit.'

'Tracksuit? Weren't you meeting Mr Golden-balls today? I thought you were going to look all hoity-toity, professional and stuff. I'm dying to hear all about it. Did you give him hell?'

'Yeah. That didn't quite work out the way I thought it would. I'll explain when I see you. You didn't ask why I can't walk.'

'Didn't need to. I was on the dance floor with you for most of the night, remember, babe? My feet are bloody killing me too. Tell you what. You go and get changed and I'll pick you up in a cab in half an hour. Bruce can pay for that, too. After all, he was the one in charge of that ace disco last night, so it's all his fault. See ya.'

Ali grinned. Anyone would think Jules didn't love Bruce, but the truth was, she loved him to bits and he felt the same about her. Of course, their soon-to-happen marriage probably wouldn't last. Any more than Sasha and John's marriage would. Which was a pity really because they were all such lovely people. When Jules wasn't in Bridezilla mode and a complete and utter nightmare, that is.

Ali gingerly made her way upstairs, spent fifteen luxurious minutes in a lavender scented bath before rapidly throwing on a pair of black trousers and a floral shirt, together with a pair of toe-post, mule-heeled sandals, which again, had cost her mum a fortune. They were like sinking her feet into a pillow of air, so today they were worth any price, no matter how high.

She grabbed her keys from the no longer cherished wooden bowl just as a car horn beeped outside.

'I'm going out with Jules and Sasha,' she yelled to the both firmly closed doors of the study and the dining room and dashed out the front door as fast as her painful feet would allow, before her parents had time to reply.

'So what was the row about this time?' Jules asked, as Ali climbed in beside her on the rear seat of the cab.

'Mum not wanting to sit on the floor to eat, I think. Although with those two these days, it could've been about anything.'

Sasha sniggered from the other side of Jules. 'I can't see Aunt Tabitha sitting on the floor, crossed leg with a plate on her lap.'

'She'd rather die,' Ali said. 'She's having a dinner party and Dad's decided to book the removers for the day before. It's his parents' dining table and chairs, so he's taking them, which sort of leaves Mum in the lurch. She's repeatedly said how busy she is at work at the moment, so finding replacement dining furniture and having it delivered in time is a big problem. She thinks he's planned it because he knew about the dinner weeks ago. The entire street knew about it. I'm surprised there wasn't a notice in The Times, or at least the local paper. She made a real fuss about who would and wouldn't be coming. Dad wasn't invited, needless to say and to quote Mum's words to me: "It's to welcome the new partner, Alejandro to the fold and he's an absolute dish himself. I wouldn't mind making a meal of him, if you follow my meaning, darling." That was said at full volume and the town crier probably thought he'd be out of a job. Dad was in his study at the time, so he definitely got the message loud and clear.'

'Has he done it on purpose?' Jules asked. 'Booked the removers, I mean.'

'Probably. I think they go to bed each night in their rooms at opposite ends of the house, and plan how to score as many points over one another as they possibly can and what to do to make each other thoroughly pissed off. But what they don't seem to realise, is how this is affecting other people. And by that, I mainly mean me, of course. Hmm. Sometimes I wonder if I'm as selfish as Mum.'

Jules gave her a hug. 'You're not at all selfish, babe. You're always doing things for others no matter how time consuming or difficult they might be. Especially for your friends. You're always ready, willing and able to help out a friend. Particularly your best friend.'

'Why do I get the feeling you want me to do something for you, Jules? Is that why you phoned and asked me to join you? Oh, don't give me that look. I've seen it too often. What is it? Or do you want to wait until I have a drink in my hand before you ask?'

Sasha gave a burst of laughter. 'You'll need more than one drink when you hear what Jules wants.'

'That bad?'

Jules tutted. 'No. It's only a tiny thing really. And it'll wash out.'

'Wash out? That's a bit worrying. What, exactly, will wash out?'

The cab pulled up outside The Golden Dragon. 'That'll be a fiver exactly, my lovelies,' the driver said. 'Want me to add it to Bruce's account?'

'Yes please, babe,' Jules confirmed. 'And add a 50p tip for yourself.'

'So?' Ali said, once they had piled out and were standing on the pavement. 'What will wash out?'

Jules linked one arm through Ali's and one through Sasha's. 'Semi-permanent hair colour.' The three of them pushed open the double doors of the pub.

'Semi-permanent what? Are you saying you want me to dye my hair for you?'

'Semi-permanently, yes. Don't look so worried. I want everything matching for my wedding. The bridesmaids' dresses, shoes, bags, hair. Sasha's up for it and I'll have to bleach hers because getting dark brown hair to go the exact shade of Strawberry Blonde I want won't be easy unless it's on a bleached base. Your shade of natural blonde hair will take the colour without a problem. Then it'll wash right out after a few times and you won't even remember you changed the colour at all.'

'You changed the colour, you mean. May I think about it?'

'Of course. I wasn't planning to do it until Monday evening.'

'Monday evening?' Ali leant on the bar. 'This Monday evening? Tomorrow?'

'Yes.' Jules waved a perfectly manicured hand at Ronnie, the barman. 'Three G&Ts please, babe. And have one yourself. On Bruce's tab, naturally.'

Ronnie grinned. 'Hair of the dog? I'm surprised you three are still standing. Ace party, by the way, Sasha.'

Sasha beamed at him. 'Thanks, Ronnie. And thanks again for working the bar.'

'Enjoyed every minute of it.' He winked and poured their drinks.

Jules nodded towards an unoccupied table and they all headed in that direction.

'So why Monday?' Ali dumped her bag on a vacant chair and the others did likewise. 'You've got months until the wedding.'

Jules took a large swig of her drink and sighed. 'I needed that. I may have months, but you wouldn't believe how much I've still got to sort out. I need to make sure the colour's perfect, so the sooner we try it, the sooner I can tick that off my list.'

'You mean this is just a trial run? You may need to try another?'

Jules shrugged. 'Possibly.'

Ali shook her head. 'OK, Jules. You know I love you but you're not messing around with my hair. Once, I don't have too much of a problem with – but if it all goes horribly wrong, I'll kill you. But more than once, is a completely different matter.'

'It won't do any harm at all to your hair, I promise.'

'I'm doing it,' Sasha said, grinning into her glass. 'And I'm having bleach.'

Ali tutted and nudged Sasha with her shoulder. 'Yes, but you're an idiot and your hair has been every colour of the rainbow three times over.'

'True.' Sasha emptied her glass. 'Want another?'

'Slow down, babe,' Jules advised her, emptying her own glass and handing it over. 'Might as well make it a double. That way we won't have to go back so often.'

Ali glanced from her cousin to her friend, shrugged, and knocked back her own G&T.

'Will you do it?' Jules asked, when Sasha went to the bar.

'Do I have much choice?' Ali grinned at her friend. 'Yes I'll do it. But remember what I said. If my hair turns green, or starts falling out, or anything else, you're dead.'

'Absolutely.' Jules crossed her heart with her fingers before giving Ali a massive hug. 'Can you be at the salon by five? Or will you need to get permission from the new manager?'

Ali laughed. 'I'll ask myself if I'll let me leave early.'

'Huh?'

'I'll tell you when Sasha gets back.'

They only had to wait a few seconds. Apart from Sasha, there was no one else ordering drinks.

'Ali's being weird,' Jules said.

'I'm not being weird. I've been promoted. I'm now the manager of The Shimmering River and Water Sports Centre. As from today. And I get a pay rise. Which will probably only buy one G&T, but every little helps, as the saying goes.'

Shrieks of delight filled the pub and Ronnie gave them a questioning look.

'Ali's got the job,' Jules informed him.

'The manager's job? Good on you, girl.' Ronnie raised a glass. 'Cheers!'

'Yes, cheers!' Jules and Sasha repeated.

'Thank you.'

'So how the hell did that happen?' Sasha asked. 'I thought the boss' son was the new manager.'

'He was. But at our meeting today, he gave the job to me. And I'll tell you something else.' She leant forward conspiratorially. 'He's bloody gorgeous, so I'm kind of hoping that's not the only thing he might give me.'

'Ali!' Jules and Sasha looked at one another and then stared at her.

'Seriously?' Jules queried. 'I thought you hated everything his family stands for.'

'I do. But apparently that doesn't stop me fancying the pants off him. You just wait till you see him. That man who plays Poldark on the telly pales to nothing compared to Aidan Rourke. Talk about takes your breath away... I couldn't breathe, I couldn't think, I couldn't move. All I could do was sit there and lust after him. He must think I'm a complete idiot.'

Sasha shook her head. 'Then he won't be the only one. You can't possibly fall for a guy who is so damn rich that all he does is lead the life of a playboy. When he and his family aren't demolishing perfectly good buildings, or replacing reasonably priced leisure centres with exclusive clubs and ripping everyone off in the process. No matter how gorgeous he looks in a photo.'

'You've seen his photo?' Ali was surprised. 'Why didn't you show me? At least then I wouldn't have been so gobsmacked when he walked in.'

Sasha pulled a face. 'I thought you'd checked him out online.'

'I checked out his dad and the companies they own. I don't remember seeing any photos of Aidan.'

'I could only find a couple. Anyone would think the guy doesn't actually want his photo taken.'

'Probably because he'd have thousands of female stalkers if he did. I'm not kidding you. I have never in my life seen a man as gorgeous as him.'

Jules shifted in her seat. 'And you've got to work with him?'

'I'm not really sure. He told me that he was leaving the place in my hands but that he would be popping in from time to time. And then, get this, he leant forward, all sexy-like and said in a voice that alone could make you orgasm: "and now that I know what this place has to offer, I'll be popping in a lot more", or something along those lines. To be honest I was so busy trying not to grab him, throw him on the desk and jump on top of him, that I didn't hear exactly what he said.'

'Oh my God!' Sasha knocked back her drink. 'I need another. If that was a double, I'm a Ninja Princess.'

'Keep drinking like that, babe,' Jules said, downing hers. 'And you probably will be. At least, in your imagination.'

Ali shook her head. 'I can't keep up with you two. I'm OK with mine.'

'Slacker.' Sasha headed towards the bar yet again and returned with three more G&Ts.

'I said I was fine,' Ali complained.

'Save it for later, babe,' Jules said. 'Bruce is paying.'

'I almost feel sorry for your fiancé.'

Jules smiled. 'So do I. Sometimes. But then I realise how lucky he is to have me.'

'Oooh! I forgot.' Ali slapped the palm of her hand on the table. 'I think Simon proposed to me this morning.' A spray of liquid hit her in the face. 'Oh God, Sasha! You just spat your drink all over me.'

'Sorry.' Sasha swiped her hand across her mouth. 'But bloody hell, Ali. You can't come out with something like that and not expect a reaction.'

'Sasha's right.' Jules was clearly stunned. 'Simon proposed? To you? Was he drunk?'

Ali wiped her face with a tissue from her handbag and threw the tissue at Sasha. 'Yeah. Thanks for the vote of confidence. But seriously. I'm pretty sure he was joking. He said he was. And it wasn't so much a proposal, as a suggestion. The thing is … it sort of got me thinking.'

'About marrying Simon?' Sasha shrieked.

'God no! About exactly what his feelings are for me. I mean, we've always been really good friends. Best friends. I talk to him about the same things we talk about.'

'What menstrual cramps and bikini waxes?' Jules joked. 'Having sex with guys?'

'Oh, very funny. Although, I think I have discussed menstrual cramps with him.'

'Jesus Christ.' Jules rolled her eyes. 'I bet he found that fascinating.'

'He didn't seem to mind. Anyway, we're getting off topic. The point I'm making is, is he harbouring feelings for me? Or was it the alcohol from last night?'

Jules and Sasha exchanged looks and nodded simultaneously. 'Alcohol.'

'He's known you too long to suddenly get the hots for you,' Jules said. 'It might be different if you'd been fat and lost a lot of weight, or something. You know? Like in those films where the girls have been hit by the ugly stick then suddenly turn into drop-dead gorgeous bombshells overnight. But you haven't changed one bit in all the years he's known you.'

'She's grown boobs and got a waist since she was two,' Sasha pointed out. 'Oh, and grown several feet in height. But yeah, no change other than that.'

'Really?' Ali peered at her friends. 'No change? Nothing?'

Sasha rubbed Ali's arm. 'Hey. That's a good thing. Change is highly overrated.'

'Well, look at it like this,' Jules said, emptying her glass once more. 'You will be changing tomorrow. From tomorrow night, you'll no longer be a plain, white blonde. You'll be a stunningly, Strawberry Blonde. I think we should drink to that. Oh bugger. I think there's a hole in my glass. I'd better get another one.'

Ali sighed. This was going to be a long evening. And tomorrow, she'd have Strawberry Blonde hair. What would Aidan Rourke think of that? Or would it have washed out before he got a chance to see it?

Chapter Five

Ali trusted Jules with most things but as she sat in one of the purple chairs in Shimmering Scissors Hair and Beauty, she was shaking. Actually shaking. It didn't help that every song playing on the radio since she arrived had been about people making mistakes, and the fact that they were about things going wrong in relationships, not at the hairdressers, didn't make any difference to Ali's premonition of doom.

'Trust me,' Jules said, tying the purple gown at the nape of Ali's neck. 'What could possibly go wrong?'

'You're asking me?' Ali's fingers gripped the arms of the chair.

'What I meant was, nothing will go wrong, babe. I've done this thousands of times.'

For some reason that wasn't very comforting. 'Planes take off and land thousands of times – but sometimes they crash.'

'Seriously, Ali? You're likening having your hair coloured, semi-permanently let's not forget, to a plane crash?'

'It's going to be Strawberry Blonde. That's flame-like. Strawberries are bright red.'

Jules shook her head. 'I wonder about you sometimes, babe. It'll be fine. Drink your coffee and eat the biscuit. You're in safe hands.'

'I bet that's what Sweeny Todd, the demon barber, said to his customers.'

'If you don't shut it, you bloody well will end up in a pie. If you don't want to do this you've only got to say so. I mean, it's only my wedding we're talking about. It's not like it's anything important, is it?' Jules' voice hit fever-pitch.

'OK. I'm sorry. It's simply that I've never coloured my hair before. Ever. I think my hair is the one really attractive thing about me and forgive me if I'm feeling just a little bit scared of losing my one real asset.'

'Rubbish,' Sasha said. She was sitting in the chair next to Ali and her hair was slowly turning a pale pink before Ali's eyes. 'You've got good legs, a nice bum, your eyes are lovely and, um, your boobs aren't bad. Not brilliant, but not too shabby either.'

'High praise indeed. Thanks, Sasha.'

'Was that sarcasm? Because I'm only trying to help, you know.'

'Sorry. I know you are. I'm terrified, that's all. But I do trust Jules, so let's get on with this.' She reached out for the biscuit and dunked it in her coffee.

Jules placed her hands on Ali's shoulders. 'You sure?'

'I'm sure,' Ali said, through a mouthful of soggy chocolate digestive.

Jules walked over to an alcove as Ali watched in the large oval mirror hanging on the purple and gold, papered walls in front of her chair. Daisy, Jules' assistant had put some bottles on a worktop and Ali could see Jules pouring liquid from three of them into a bowl and stirring vigorously with a long slim paintbrush-like tool. Moments later, Jules returned with the bowl which now contained a soup of bright orange-looking goo. Ali sent up a silent prayer that it wasn't going to be that colour once it sunk into each and every fibre of her beautiful, white blonde hair.

A flash went off beside her. 'Just taking a photo of you as you are now,' Sasha said, smiling at Ali. 'Just in case it's the last time you'll ever be that colour.'

Ali's stomach knotted, her throat went dry and her heart pounded against her chest as she stared at Sasha. 'Thanks a lot.'

'How was your first day as manager?' Jules asked, slathering the revolting mixture onto Ali's locks.

'OK, I think. It's not going to be that colour when it dries, is it?'

'Nope. What do you mean, you think? Weren't the other staff pleased? I thought they all felt you should've got the job in the first place.'

'They did. And yes, they were pleased. We were going to pop out for a quick drink to celebrate but we thought better of it in case Aidan turned up unannounced. I nipped out and bought a couple of bottles of bubbly instead and we had a few glasses before I came here.'

'Why didn't we think of that?' Sasha asked Jules. 'Could we send Daisy out to get some before she leaves for the evening?'

'That's a good idea.' Jules disappeared into another room via a purple, open door and reappeared with Daisy following behind her.

Daisy smiled at them and jogged towards the glass door of the salon. 'Back in a mo.'

'So, did Gorgeous-balls show his handsome face?' Jules asked, plastering on more of the goo until Ali's hair stuck firmly to her head.

'Sadly not. But perhaps he wanted to give me space and time to tell the staff – all ten of them. He's probably leaving us to it for a few days and then he'll turn up and do a spot check or something. We're simply carrying on as normal. It's pretty quiet this week, but when the school holidays start, things will really pick up. The dormitory is full from next week onwards until virtually the end of the summer and we've got a few other groups booked for sailing, kayaking, windsurfing and kite surfing. Then there's the wake boarding and, of course, water skiing. It'll be all go. But I like it when it's like that. It's the quiet times I don't like so much, when we're all sitting around doing nothing.'

'But there's always something going on throughout the year,' Sasha said. 'It's a shame you can't boost the quieter months even more by arranging other activities.'

'That's actually one of the things we were discussing today. Ways to do just that. We haven't come up with anything yet but there's plenty of time. I hope.'

'Why hope?' Jules asked. 'Do you think the Rourkes have other plans?'

'No idea. It's simply an odd feeling I have, that's all. It's probably nothing.'

'I think you'll find that feeling is lust,' Sasha said, grinning. 'You probably don't remember what that's like because it's been so long since you had sex with anyone, but you're lusting after Aidan.'

'You're not wrong there. D'you know, when I got to my office this morning all I could think about was the way he was sitting on my desk yesterday and the way his eyes seemed to be telling me that they'd be seeing a lot more of me – if you get my meaning.'

'Oh we get it, babe,' Jules said, as Daisy burst in through the door with a bottle of bubbly in each hand and another tucked under her arm. The convenience store was only two doors away but she must have run like an Olympian to make it there and back so fast.

'Will three be enough?' Daisy asked. 'That's all they had in the shop.'

'I suppose it'll have to be.' Jules nodded towards the other room. 'Grab some glasses will you, babe? They're in the cupboard in there. Top shelf. You'll join us for a drink or two, won't you?'

Daisy hesitated. 'Thanks. I'd love to but I can't. My boyfriend's picking me up and I saw his car as I was coming in the door. I'll get your glasses and then, if it's OK, can I dash off?'

'You go,' Sasha said, getting up. 'I'll get the glasses. Don't worry, Jules, I won't drip onto your floor.'

'My hair colourant doesn't drip, thank you very much.'

'Thanks. Bye. Have a brill time,' Daisy said, and was gone before anyone had time to reply.

Sasha got the glasses and poured the drinks. 'Here's to Ali's promotion, and to the future, whatever it may hold. Cheers.'

They all clinked glasses and drank. Jules brought out more digestives and they nibbled those and drank some more.

'Ooh!' Jules said, with a mouthful of biscuit. 'I almost forgot. Have you spoken to Simon today?'

Ali nodded. 'Yeah. Just briefly. I felt a bit crap when he called. I usually tell him everything and I was going to call him yesterday to tell him about the promotion, but then you phoned and we went to the pub. You'd said he'd be joining us so I waited to tell him face-to-face, but then of course he didn't show up. I was a bit the worse for wear and still shattered from the party so ... well, in a nutshell, I hadn't told him I was promoted to manager and he was a bit pissed off that he was the last to know, especially as he'd left me a couple of messages and all I'd done was sent a text saying: 'Went better than expected. Will see you soon to tell you all.' He did at least have the decency to congratulate me and he suggested we go out to celebrate tonight, but I told him I was having my hair done and he went all weird and said something along the lines of: 'Fine. Call me when you're free and we'll do something then.' And rang off. I got the impression he wasn't happy, so I'll have to make it up to him, I suppose.'

'I bet he's not,' Sasha said. 'He's usually the first person you tell when you have news, whether it's good or bad.'

'I know. And that's why I felt crap. But since that proposal joke and me meeting the gorgeous, demi-god, Aidan, something's changed, I think. It's as if ... oh, I don't know. It's like something's come between us. I'm sure it's nothing and we'll be back to the way we've always been in a week or so. At least I hope we will. I can't imagine not having him as my best friend.'

'One of your best friends, you mean, babe. Let's not forget about me.'

Ali smiled at her. 'No one could ever forget about you, Jules.'

'Anyway, that's not why I asked.' Jules poured more Prosecco into their glasses. 'Did he mention the cruise?'

'Cruise? What cruise?'

'Is Simon going on a cruise?' Sasha piped up.

Jules shook her head. 'Not Simon, no. His mum.'

Ali's mouth fell open. 'Maggie doesn't go on holiday. Well, not unless Simon goes with her, or for a day out or something as a treat, or to visit relatives up north. If she's going on a cruise – which I frankly doubt – then Simon must be going too. The only place she goes without him, is to visit her sister-in-law every couple of months in Norfolk, and even then, Simon drives her there and picks her up again.'

'Wrong!' Jules grinned triumphantly. 'For once I know more about Simon than you do. Maggie told me herself, so I got it from the horse's mouth. She came in this morning for her weekly cut and blow-dry and she's booked a cruise. But Simon did help, which is why he didn't come to the pub yesterday because they booked it online and she's crap with the internet, she says, so he had to do it all for her. They spent hours looking at various cruise lines and destinations but they eventually found one and booked it. Oh, and she's going with the sister-in-law you mentioned. They Skyped one another about it, or something. I didn't catch all of it because the hairdryers in here were going, and Maggie does chatter-on, doesn't she?'

Ali banged her glass down. 'And he got stroppy because I hadn't told him about the promotion. Bloody cheek. You wait until I see him. He didn't even mention it.'

Jules and Sasha exchanged glances.

'Something weird has definitely happened between you two,' Sasha said, shaking her head in a doom-like fashion.

'Yeah,' Jules added. 'Really weird. But on the up side. Simon might not be such a mummy's boy in future.'

'Simon's *not* a mummy's boy.'

'OK. No need to bite my head off.'

'Jules does have a point,' Sasha said. 'The guy is almost thirty-five and he still lives with his mum. Don't get me wrong, we all love him, but still. He needs to get a life. I don't even think he's had that many girlfriends, has he?'

'He's had ten in the past fifteen years.' Ali grabbed another bottle of Prosecco from Jules, who was struggling with the cork, and popped it for her. 'But he always seems to pick the wrong type of women, so they never last. And it's Maggie who can't cope without Simon, not the other way around. That's why she had her house converted into flats. So that he would always be close by. I tried to tell him at the time that it might not be the best idea to go along with, but he said he couldn't simply move out and leave her in the lurch. He's got such a good heart.'

Jules opened her mouth, glanced at Ali, then at Sasha and quickly closed it.

'What?' Ali glared at her. 'Come on, say it. We're all friends here.'

'Um. It wasn't Maggie who had the house converted. It was Simon. Didn't he tell you? That's one of the things I did hear her tell me today. She was so excited about the cruise that it all came tumbling out. People often tell hairdressers things they shouldn't.'

'What? She told you that Simon did it?'

Jules nodded. 'Uh-huh. He bought the place from her, you must know that, at least, and then he paid for it to be converted. He wanted his own space but he also wanted to be close to her in case anything happened. It seemed the perfect solution. That's why I said he was a mummy's boy, but she did admit that she keeps forgetting he's a grown up and not her baby. She said she's been a little slow in giving him the space he needs. That's why she's decided to go on the cruise. She and Sam always planned to cruise when they retired, but of course he dropped down dead, so that put a spanner in the works.'

Ali couldn't speak but Sasha did. 'Bloody hell. He kept that quiet. Where did he get the money to buy her out and then convert the place? That house must be worth a few hundred-thousand. He couldn't get that sort of mortgage on a teacher's salary.'

'Oh he didn't.' Jules now seemed to be the font of all Simon-related knowledge. 'He's got investments, apparently. His dad left him a share of some company or other, and there's other money that's been invested since the day of Simon's birth. He's worth a substantial amount of money, so Maggie said. Not as rich as your new boss, but certainly not the poor teacher I always thought he was. Are you OK, Ali? You've gone a funny colour. And it has nothing to do with my hair colourants before you say it has.'

'I … I didn't know any of this.' Ali was struggling to take in everything Jules had revealed. 'He did tell me that his dad had left him an inheritance, made up of some small investments or something, but he didn't say it was worth anything. And he definitely didn't tell me about the house and the conversion being his idea or that he had bought and paid for it all. I … I thought we told each other everything. All our secrets. All our plans. Well, what a fool I've been. It seems I was the only one spilling my guts whilst he was keeping his whole life a secret from me.'

'I think that's a bit of an exaggeration,' Sasha said. 'But perhaps he had good reason. He knows your mum. We all do. If she'd known Simon had money, she'd have married the two of you off years ago – and then acted for you in the divorce and left him penniless.'

71

'Yeah. And perhaps he wanted to be liked for who he is, not what he's got. Are you wishing that his proposal had been genuine now?' Jules asked. 'Or kicking yourself for not taking it seriously, if it was?'

'Neither. I'm bloody furious that he's lied to me all these years. Does he think his money would've made any difference to me? He knows how I feel about the whole marriage thing because, unlike him, I've been open and honest throughout our entire friendship. Well, some bloody friend he is if all he does is keep secrets. He can damn well sod off. And take his money with him.'

They all fell silent and focussed their attention on their drinks until Jules let out a little cough after several seconds. 'And on that note, I think it's about time I washed the colour off your hair.'

Sasha went first because hers was first on and she was followed to the row of four sinks, by Ali, who sat, quietly contemplating what had just happened. Jules chattered away whilst washing Sasha's hair, clearly attempting to lighten the now sombre mood and, after more Prosecco and a handful of chocolate digestives, Ali wasn't feeling quite so hopeless about it all.

By the time it was her turn, she was in a far better mood. She would have it out with Simon and tell him how disappointed she was, and, provided he didn't make excuses and simply told her the truth now, she would possibly forgive him. Men were different to women. They didn't feel the

72

need to tell their friends everything. It wasn't lying, exactly. It was more like keeping their own counsel. She and Simon could still be friends. But it wouldn't be the same. Things had definitely changed. A day really can make a difference. A huge difference.

Perhaps that wasn't such a bad thing. Simon always got a bit weird when she had a boyfriend and as she would soon, hopefully, be spending more time with Aidan, Simon would've given her a bit of the cold-shoulder treatment anyway. He was always there with a shoulder to cry on when things went south on the boyfriend front. But perhaps she wouldn't need him this time. Perhaps Aidan was 'the one'. Not that she would marry him or anything. But they could live together, possibly. That might not be so bad. Except she would always need Simon around. She couldn't really imagine her life without him in it.

'Sit here,' Jules said, indicating the chair Sasha had just vacated, and Ali did so, with a smile. The relief on Jules' face was evident. 'For a minute there, I thought I'd caused the third World War or something. I thought you'd known about it all along and simply hadn't told us. Sorry if I've ruined your day.'

'You haven't ruined my day. Hmmmm. That feels good,' Ali said, as Jules washed the colour off and massaged Ali's scalp, adding shampoo and then conditioner.

'I love having my scalp massaged,' Jules said. 'I'm trying to teach Bruce how to do it but the man's hopeless at it. Which is odd because he's pretty damn good with his hands in other ways. What he can do … oh holy shit!'

Jules' chattering came to an abrupt halt and Ali glanced up from her position on the reclining chair to see an ashen look on her friend's face, and eyebrows raised so high they nearly disappeared into Jules' hairline.

'Oh my God, Jules. What's happened? What's wrong?'

'Now I don't want you to worry, Ali, because it's not the end of the world. And we can probably fix it with a bit of peroxide and another semi-permanent tint. Only this one definitely wasn't the semi-permanent one. And it wasn't even the right colour. Bit of a cock-up it seems. But copper-mahogany definitely suits you and once you get used to it, you might even come to love it. Besides, it's good to have a change. This could be a whole new start for you. Goodbye to the old Ali. Welcome to the new, improved Ali, who embraces life and change and still loves her friends, no matter what they do.'

Chapter Six

Simon was having a crappy Monday. He couldn't remember the last time he'd felt like this. At least his mum was happy, that was some consolation. Although her advice to 'give Ali a little time and she'll forget you proposed and made a bit of a hash of it,' had back-fired, somewhat. And he clearly wouldn't get the chance to 'do it properly next time'. Not that he wanted there to be a next time. He was crazy to have proposed. He hadn't really meant it. Not really. He was simply feeling strange about he and Ali being the only ones from their circle of friends who weren't engaged or married, and it seemed like a good idea at the time. What concerned him was whether he should say anything to Ali to explain, or whether he should let the matter drop. The last thing on his mind was how to do it properly next time. And he had to face it. It was now abundantly clear there wasn't going to be a next time anyway.

He always thought he and Ali told each other everything. He thought he was the first person she called when she had good news. He was definitely the first one she called when there was bad. But she'd got the promotion she'd wanted and had she called to tell him? No. She'd gone to the pub with Jules and Sasha instead and hadn't even texted him to tell him to join them.

OK, so Jules had already told him they were going to the pub when he'd bumped into her as she was coming out of her flat above her salon, and he was buying a Sunday newspaper, but that wasn't the point. If the paper hadn't had a large travel section in it, and this week, an extra Travel Magazine, he wouldn't have been there buying it, and then he wouldn't have known they were going to the pub. He'd only bought the paper after he and his mum had had a heart to heart and she'd decided he was right. It was time she grabbed life by the horns and went on that cruise she and his dad had always dreamed of.

Perhaps Ali assumed he'd meet them at the pub? Perhaps Jules had said she'd seen him? Even so, Ali should have called. When he had finally spoken to her today, all she could talk about was how nice this Aidan guy was and how thoughtful and considerate. How he wasn't the ogre she'd imagined but more like a demi-god or something.

Sodding demi-god. He knew what Ali meant by that. It meant she had the hots for this guy and that meant trouble for Simon. It meant he'd spend his days and nights worrying if things were going well. Wondering if the guy was good in bed. Hoping that, as always, the relationship would end before too long – and yet at the same time, wanting her to be happy. Wanting her to finally fall in love. Wanting it to be with someone he thought understood her. Wanting it to be with someone who wouldn't object to Ali and Simon being friends. Who wouldn't try to block him out of Ali's life. Who wouldn't…

Oh shit.

Why didn't he simply admit it? To himself, at least.

He wanted it to be him.

Chapter Seven

Aidan sat in a leather chair in his dad's sumptuous study, nursing a large Scotch whilst his dad stared out the window towards the swimming pool and private 18-hole golf course surrounded by woods beyond.

'It went well then?' Greg Rourke asked.

Aidan smiled, even though his father wasn't looking at him. 'I think so. I had a proper look around the place and it's perfect. Exactly what we'd expected.'

'And this girl? The one you've promoted to manager. What's she like? Apart from being, "a blonde bombshell" as you said.' Greg turned to his son and grinned. 'I've no objection to you mixing business with pleasure, son, you know that. But will she give us any trouble?'

Aidan tipped his head to one side. 'No. I don't think she will. She's got a good body – I could tell that even covered by the old tracksuit she was wearing – but she's no genius. She hardly said a word the entire time I was there. If the previous owner hadn't told us she was so good at her job, I'd have thought she was a bit dim and a complete waste of space. Well, on the work front anyway. On a personal level, I think she'll be a lot of fun.'

'So we'll go ahead as planned?'

Aidan nodded and took a swig of his Scotch. 'We still need to sort out the purchase of that other piece of land. I can't believe those bloody lawyers screwed that up. Then we'll file the pre-planning application to see for certain how things lie on that front. If all goes well, we'll knock the place down and build as many luxury homes as quickly and as cheaply as possible.'

'And for now?'

'I think I might spend a little time, shall we say, doing some groundwork.'

Greg gave a hoot of laughter. 'You're a chip off the old block, my boy. There's no denying that. I hope she doesn't disappoint.'

'She's blonde, a few years younger than me, clearly hopeless with men, if the way she reacted to me was anything to go by, single, and not very bright. What's not to like? She won't retain my interest for long, I'm absolutely certain of that, but a few days of sun, sailing and sex is no bad thing.'

'If she's got a sister, I might be tempted to join you. You'll find the older you get, my boy, the younger you want your women to be. Although eighteen's the limit. Younger than that, and you're in trouble. Don't even go there.'

'I don't intend to.'

'When do you plan to go back?'

'I thought I'd give them a few days to settle. Perhaps Friday. I could go down for the weekend. Take the yacht. Unless you're using it.'

'No. It's Monte Carlo for me. There's a wealthy old woman staying there, whose daughter I've taken quite a fancy to and whose English stately home is virtually falling down. I'm hoping to get my hands on both the estate and the daughter this weekend. There's also a table in the casino, with my name on it.' He grinned and held his empty glass in the air. 'Another?'

Aidan smiled in admiration, got up from his chair and walked towards the 1930s cocktail cabinet, inlaid with pearls and trimmed with gold, purchased, together with the large English estate of a former Hollywood star, during another of his dad's weekends away.

Chapter Eight

'Your hair looks lovely, Ali-ba-ba. That colour really suits you.' Gertie, Ali's maternal grandmother hovered in the doorway of the dining room when Ali opened the front door of the Warner family home. 'You look as pretty as a picture. But why the long face, my angel?'

Gertie's cheery, throaty voice always made Ali smile, no matter what her mood. 'Thanks, Gertie. It's so lovely to see you. I was going to pop round tomorrow for a natter and some of your scrumptious cake.'

'Tabby-cat's been telling me you got the promotion you wanted. Congratulations!'

Tabitha gave Gertie an icy glare. 'How many times must I ask you, mother? Please don't call me Tabby-cat? I'm a fifty-nine-year-old, successful lawyer, not a five-year-old urchin.'

Gertie chuckled as Ali hugged her. 'You'll always be my little urchin. You were a lovely child. Shame you grew up to be so angry at the world. Don't you even have a kind word and a kiss for your own daughter who looks like she needs all the hugs she can get, despite her beautiful hair and super-duper new job.'

'I'm not angry at the world. I'm angry at that good-for-nothing husband of mine. Soon to be ex-husband, thankfully. And at you for persisting in berating me, instead of showing me some support.'

'I'm here, aren't I? Though I don't know why. You've hardly said a word to me since I arrived. I even had to pour my own G&T and I suppose I'll have to pour myself another.'

Tabitha snatched at Gertie's empty, crystal glass before smiling wanly at Ali. 'Hello darling. How was your day?' She pulled Ali to her and gave her a perfunctory hug. 'I need a drink. You?'

'Er, no thanks. I had a few glasses of Prosecco at Jules'.' She watched her mum walk into the dining room. 'Aren't you going to say anything about my hair, Mum?'

Tabitha turned back to look at her. 'What's happened to it? Oh good heavens! Have you dyed it? Are those highlights? Copper mahogany and gold? Was that wise? Don't tell me Jules did that.'

'She did. It was supposed to be Strawberry Blonde – and semi-permanent – but it went a bit wrong.'

'I think it looks lovely,' Gertie said, giving Ali another brief hug.

'You would,' Tabitha responded.

'It suits her.'

Tabitha stared at Ali before turning away and pouring three large G&Ts. She added ice and sliced a lemon from the bowl of lemons and limes on the cocktail cabinet, dropping one slice in each glass. Carrying them deftly between her fingers, she handed each of them a glass.

'I said I didn't want one.' Ali took it anyway.

'You may need it. I've got something to tell you. That's why I got Gertie here.'

That sounded ominous.

'And I thought it was to spend some time with a mother you loved. Silly me.'

Tabitha ignored Gertie's remark and continued: 'Let's go into the sitting room. As much as I'm loathe to admit it, Gertie's right about your hair. It does suit you, darling, although I'm still unsure about the colour. I can categorically agree it's not Strawberry Blonde.' She nodded and, to Ali's complete surprise, kissed her on the cheek. 'Yes. It definitely brings out the colour of your eyes. I've always loved your eyes. They're just like your … oh, but we won't go there. His eyes are what got me into this mess in the first place.' She marched into the room and plonked herself on one of the large, plush, white sofas.

'Your attitude is what got you into this mess,' Gertie said, easing herself down into a matching armchair. 'Tom's eyes made you fall in love. Your constant need to be better than everyone else is what made you unhappy. Look at this house. Eight

83

bedrooms? For the three of you? Insanity, that's what that is.'

'We bought this house for the views. And the space. And my attitude is what got me to be made a partner of one of the most prestigious law firms in the City.'

'As nutty as a fruitcake, that's what you are, Tabby-cat. Partner of a law firm indeed. All that's got you is long hours, a long commute, and a long face, smothered in premature wrinkles. Look at me. My face is still as bright as a button and I'm almost eighty-five. I don't need any of those eye-bogglingly expensive creams and potions that cover every inch of your fancy dressing table. No wonder Tom hasn't held you in his arms for ages. You probably kept slipping right out, you're so covered in grease and goo. You're as slippery as an eel.'

'And you're a mad old woman. That simile doesn't mean slippery in that sense, it means untrustworthy, a shady character.'

Gertie laughed. 'And?'

'I don't know why I bother.'

'You don't bother. That's your problem.'

Ali stood in the doorway and watched them. She loved her gran, even if Gertie did insist on being called Gertie, not Gran. She loved her mum, too. But listening to them both made her want to cry. Gertie was so kind and loving towards Ali, yet she was sometimes unkind to her own daughter. Ali couldn't remember it always being like this though. They all used to be happy. They all hugged and kissed and really cared for one another.

Things had been going downhill in her parents' relationship for some time, but Ali had tried to ignore it in the hope that it was just a phase. A phase they would get through. She hated the fact that her once-loving parents were almost constantly at each other's throats. Now it seemed, without her even noticing, the relationship between her mum and her gran had gone the same way. It really broke her heart, and without the slightest warning, she burst into a flood of tears.

To her surprise, both her mum and her gran were at her side in an instant, wrapping their arms around her and leading her to one of the sofas.

'Sit down, darling and tell me what's wrong,' Tabitha said.

'What is it, my angel? What's happened to make you so sad?' Gertie coaxed.

'What's brought on these tears?' Tabitha asked, stroking Ali's face with an exceptionally soft-skinned hand.

Ali shook her head and between sobs, managed: 'Everything. … You and Dad and this divorce. … You and Gertie arguing. … Everyone arguing. … Simon proposing. Simon lying. … Aidan being gorgeous and not an ogre, after all. … My hair. … Everything.' She took the tissue Gertie proffered, wiped her eyes and blew her nose.

'Did you say Simon proposed?' Tabitha asked, clearly shocked. 'Our Simon?'

'He's not 'our Simon' and yes. Although I think he was joking. Or drunk. I'm not completely sure. And trust you to pick up on that out of all of it.' She blew her nose again.

'Only because it was such a surprise, darling. I had no idea he cared for you in that way. What makes you think it was a joke? And when was this? At Sasha's engagement party?'

Ali nodded.

'I always thought that young man was hiding his light beneath a bushel,' Gertie said.

Tabitha tutted but didn't comment.

'He was hiding more than a light,' Ali said. 'He was hiding the fact that he owns his mum's house. That he was the one who suggested the conversion and that he was the one who paid for it. I bet he's hiding lots of other things, too. I thought we told each other everything.'

'I thought so too, darling. But never mind. And what's this about Aidan being gorgeous? Is that Aidan Rourke? The one who promoted you. You didn't mention anything about his looks.'

'Because you weren't listening. I wasn't even sure you heard me say I'd been promoted. All you said was "Wonderful. Must dash." You never listen to me anymore.'

'I said congratulations. … Didn't I?'

'No, Mum. You didn't.'

'I meant to. I'm so sorry, my darling.' She kissed Ali on the forehead. 'Oh dear. My mother's right. I have become a selfish old bag. I'm so upset about turning sixty soon, and all this business with your father, I've completely forgotten about everyone else.'

'Hallelujah!' Gertie said. 'Light has dawned.'

Tabitha shifted her position on the sofa so that she could hold both one of Ali's hands, and one of Gertie's. 'I'm sorry. Truly sorry. Although, you could be a bit kinder to me, yourself, Mum.'

Gertie pulled a face in agreement. 'I could. There's no denying that. It comes to something when the youngest of we three is the wisest of us.'

'There's nothing wise about me,' Ali said. 'I let my best friend lie to me and I didn't even know it, and my other best friend colour my hair, even though I absolutely knew something would go wrong.'

'But it really does suit you, darling. I mean that.'

'Tabitha's right, my angel. You look even prettier than you did before. And you've always been a real beauty.'

'Well I've been hiding *that* under a bushel.'

'There's not much I can do about your father and me, darling,' Tabitha said. 'But I'll do my best with everything else. I'll be nicer to Mum. I'll listen to you whenever you want. I'm not sure I can help with either Simon or Aidan but I can be there for you when you need me, if that helps. And once you've slept on it, I think you'll see your hair is lovely. If you don't, I'll take you to the best hairstylists in London and we'll do whatever it takes to make you blonde again. Or another colour, if you prefer.'

Ali nodded and finally managed a smile. 'Thanks, Mum. Thanks, Gertie. I really love you both.'

'And we love you,' they both replied in unison.

'I may be an old fool,' Gertie said, looking at Tabitha. 'But as far as you not being able to do anything about the situation between you and Tom, I'd say that's stuff and nonsense. The question is, do you want to do anything about it? The pair of you were madly in love once. And that wasn't so long ago. You could be again.'

Tabitha let out a long, sorrowful sigh. 'There's too much water under the bridge for that. It's very sad for all of us, but people fall out of love as often as they fall into it and then fall in love with someone else.'

'Not in my day they didn't. They worked hard at their marriages, not just at their careers. You'd be surprised what difference it can make.'

'It's too late, Mum. I didn't tell you this because it bruised my ego I suppose, but Tom's got someone else. A woman half my age. Less than half my age, in fact. What does he want with a sixty-year-old, with sagging boobs, and wrinkles, when he can have a smooth skinned, pert-breasted, sex bomb hanging on his arm?'

Gertie burst out laughing. 'You're as crazy as a coot, Tabby-cat. Sorry, Tabitha. If you think Tom would leave you and Ali for a bit of fluff, then you don't know your husband at all. I'd stake my life on the fact that would be the last thing he would ever do.'

'I've seen them together. More than once. And when I asked him where he'd been, knowing he had been at a restaurant with her, he lied. He told me he'd been working late. Working late, indeed! I know an affair when I see one. It's what I get paid a fortune for.'

'Mum!' This was the first Ali had heard of another woman. Their arguments seemed to be about everything, *except* her dad having an affair. 'Did Dad admit it? And why is this the first I've heard of it?'

'Of course he didn't admit it. But I couldn't tell him I'd followed him, could I? How would that make me look? I told him I knew he was seeing someone, and I asked him to tell me who she was and whether it was serious. He denied it. Things had been a little difficult between us before that, but afterwards they obviously grew worse. I couldn't sleep with a man who was sleeping with someone else. I didn't want you to know, darling. I didn't want you to blame him. I hoped he'd eventually own up and perhaps – just perhaps – there might have been a chance for us. He didn't. And it's far too late now.'

They heard the front door open and Tom's keys rattle as he tossed them in the wooden bowl. They heard him stride along the corridor towards his study and they heard him slam the door.

'Your husband's home,' Gertie said, giving her daughter an odd look. 'Aren't you going to give him a drink and say hello?'

'No. I am not. But I am going to get another for the three of us.'

'And that, my child, is where you continue to go wrong. You're as stubborn as a mule. And I should know. You get that from me. But I've just remembered. Weren't you going to tell us something? Isn't that why you asked me here in the first place?'

The colour drained from Tabitha's face. 'Oh, yes. Yes I was.' She gave a little cough. 'I've met someone. A man, obviously. One of the partners in my firm, in fact. I'm not sure it's love, exactly, but we get on rather well and, um … I think it solves our problems. Once Tom moves out, I've asked Alejandro if he'd like to move in.'

Gertie shook her head and glared at her daughter. 'Well, that change didn't last long, did it? That's the Tabby-cat we've come to know. Putting herself and her pleasure before that of anyone else's. If you want to move in with me, my angel,' she said, tapping Ali on the knee. 'you're more than welcome. I can't imagine you'd want to stay here with a man called Alejandro and your mother romping around. Although you could move in with your father because I don't believe for a second that he is having an affair. Not one second.'

'That's right. Blame me. I think you actually prefer Tom to your own daughter. And Ali's going nowhere. This is her home and she's staying here.'

'No, I'm not! Gertie's right. I'm not living here with you and your new man. No way. Not ever. This is Dad's house as much as it is yours. Does he know anything about this?'

The door, which was ajar suddenly burst open and Tom stood in the doorway, frowning.

'What's going on? I thought it was only Tabby and I who argued in this house.'

'Well,' Gertie said, getting to her feet. 'You're in for more than one surprise, tonight, Tom. I'm going home. Ali, would you come with me, please? I could use a hand and I think your mother has something to say to your dad.'

Ali darted a look at both her parents and stood up to help her gran. 'Of course,' she said, heading towards the doorway.

'What's going on?' Tom asked again. 'What's this about? Oh. Ali. Your hair looks lovely. I really like the colour.'

He reached out and tried to hug her but she pulled away. 'Thanks, Dad. But I'm really not in the mood for father and daughter time, right now. Is it true? Are you having an affair? You two are as bad as one another.'

'Am I what? Of course I'm not. What in God's name made you think that? Oh wait. I suppose it was your mother. For the umpteenth time, would you please tell your mother that I am not, nor have I ever, had a *fucking* affair!'

'Nice going, Dad. But tell her yourself. She's sitting right there. Frankly, I'm not sure I care either way at the moment.'

Chapter Nine

'I haven't told you, have I, Ali-ba-ba? Bertie and Bonnie are getting married.'

Ali stared at her gran in disbelief. That was a joke, obviously. Gertie must've said it to try to break the silence that sat awkwardly between them as they walked, arm-in-arm, towards Gertie's house. Gertie's gait was much slower these days but as Ali's feet hadn't completely recovered from Saturday night – although the plasters one of her team had recommended were definitely helping – the snail's pace suited them both.

'Very funny, Gertie.'

Gertie stopped and threw Ali a confused look. 'Funny? Why is that funny? You know I take my little darlings to church for the animal blessings service once a month. The new vicar is very open-minded. He marries all sorts: women, men, pets. He has no objection whatsoever, provided someone in the wedding party believes in God. I don't, as you know, but your grandfather did, and as I feel he's as good as sitting on my shoulder, I'm sure that counts.'

'They're dogs, Gertie. Yorkshire Terriers. Not that their breed makes any difference.'

'You say that as if you think I don't know. I'm not senile yet, my angel. Although my darling, Tabby-cat may well drive me to it before much longer. And I mean your mother. Not that I've now got a cat.'

Ali laughed at that. 'I know who you meant. Are you serious about your dogs? Marriage? Really?'

'At least there's a good chance it won't end in divorce. Although I'm thinking of asking Tabitha to draw up a pre-nup just to annoy her. The problem with that is there's a distinct possibility she'll try to have me committed.'

'I'm considering the option myself. I know you love your dogs but …' Ali shook her head. The entire world was going mad.

'Oh it's only a bit of fun. We all need a good laugh. Especially with the current situation between your parents. And a good party. Bertie and Bonnie are going to have a wonderful wedding breakfast at Josie's. I'm having special collars made for them, too. And a wedding basket for them both to sleep in. They'll be as snug as bugs in a rug.'

'And when is this … happy event taking place?' Ali tried to stop laughing but she couldn't. This was too much.

'On Tabby-cat and Tom's wedding anniversary.' Gertie beamed at her. 'I thought that was quite appropriate. But there's a lot to do beforehand. I'm having a cake made and the wedding invitations are being printed this week. They're in the shape of a bone. I'd like you to be a bridesmaid, but if you hate the idea, that's fine – as long as you come to the wedding.'

'I wouldn't miss it for the world. That you can count on. No matter what. And I'm happy to be a bridesmaid. It may actually be fun. And I could definitely do with more of that in my life right now.'

Gertie squeezed Ali's hand, their arms still linked. 'Excellent. Everything will work out for the best, my angel. You just wait and see. Life's a bit like a river. Sometimes it meanders slowly. Sometimes it burbles with laughter even when there are rocks in its path. Sometimes it races towards the wide-open sea. And sometimes it tosses and turns and twists and leaps. But all the time, it keeps on flowing towards its destination.'

'Yeah. This Alejandro business, and Dad's supposed affair were both a bit of a shock. Especially on top of finding out Simon had kept things from me. What with everything else going on, I think my river is headed for Niagara Falls. And I'm not sure what's at the bottom.'

'Oh I've been there with your grandfather. Lovely place. It was many years ago, but I can tell you, my angel, there are rainbows at the bottom.

I've seen them. And boats full of tourists, of course.' She gave Ali's hand a second squeeze. 'Look for rainbows, Ali-ba-ba. And don't let anyone tell you they don't exist. Now, tell me about this Aidan chap. What's he like?'

'As you would probably describe him, he's as gorgeous as a summer day, and as hot as a summer night.'

'I like the sound of that.' Gertie kissed her on the cheek. 'You see, Ali-ba-ba. Rainbows, my angel. Rainbows.'

'Me too. But there's usually rain when there's a rainbow. And I'm not sure I want much more of that, metaphorically speaking, of course.'

Chapter Ten

Since the Rourkes' purchase, life at The Shimmering River and Water Sports Centre continued much as it had done before, the only difference being, that Ali was now the manager. Aidan Rourke had not put in an appearance since they had met on Sunday and as it was Tuesday, he clearly wasn't interested in her after all. That was rather disappointing. At least all the staff approved of her new hair colour. Jules had sent a flurry of apologetic texts and left a couple of voice messages, offering to do anything and everything to restore Ali's original blonde, but in truth, Ali quite liked the dark, copper red colour. A few weeks of river water, sea water and sunshine would naturally lighten it anyway.

She hadn't seen Simon since Sunday breakfast, either. The phone call on Monday was the last time she'd heard from him. She wasn't sure if he was as mad at her as she was at him. She considered calling to tell him about her mother's latest bombshell, but couldn't bring herself to press his number.

She hadn't spoken to her parents since last night. After walking back from Gertie's, she dashed upstairs to bed and locked her bedroom door. That was one thing she liked about the eight-bedroom, monstrosity of a house – the bedrooms all had locks on the doors. Why, so-called executives needed to lock their bedroom doors, whilst other people didn't, she had no idea, but at least it prevented her mum and her dad from both trying to 'have a word'. She had had enough of those from both of them.

On her way home from work, she popped into Shimmering Scissors Hair and Beauty. Jules was sweeping hair cuttings from where they had fallen on the purple and gold streaked floor. She stopped the moment she saw Ali.

'I'm so, so sorry, Ali. Are you still mad at me?'

Ali smiled at Jules, walked over to her and gave her a hug.

'Bloody hell, babe. I thought you were going to hit me for a moment. Does this mean we're friends again?'

'We never stopped being friends. I just had a bit of a temper tantrum, that's all. I'm getting more like my mum every day.'

'You're nothing like your mum. But I do remember she was lovely, once upon a time. Perhaps that's what age does to us.'

'I sincerely hope not. You haven't heard the latest. Apparently, Dad's having an affair. And Mum's got some bloke called Alejandro. He's a new partner in her firm and he's moving in as soon as Dad moves out. Won't that be fun?'

'You're kidding.'

'Sadly not. That's why I'm here. I don't suppose there's any chance I could come and stay with you for a while, is there? I would ask Sasha. But as her mum is Dad's sister, I'd rather not take sides.'

'Of course, babe. Stay for as long as you like. I should warn you, the place is a tip. There's wedding stuff everywhere. I tell you, if I wasn't such a control freak, I'd make Bruce pay for one of those wedding planner people. It's a nightmare. I'm tempted to call the whole thing off.' She grinned at Ali and nudged her arm.

'Yeah, right. You can't wait to be married to Bruce. I sometimes wish I could feel like that.'

'You can, babe.' Jules dashed into the back room, reappeared with her bag, linked her arm through Ali's and walked towards the door. 'There's plenty of time for Mr Right to come along. I know you hate the whole marriage thing, but people change. Take me for example. I used to be a complete and utter, good-time girl. Look at me now. I hardly go out at all.'

Ali laughed as they left the salon and Jules locked the door behind them.

'When do you want to move in? Tonight? Tomorrow?'

'As soon as possible, please.'

'Let's make it tonight then. We'll go to The Golden Dragon and I'll call Bruce and tell him to meet us. We'll have a drink, and after that we'll go and get your stuff.'

'Thanks Jules. I owe you one.'

'After what I did to your hair, it's the least I can do. But I still think it looks really lovely.'

'So do I, to tell you the truth.'

They walked the few metres to The Golden Dragon and, still laughing over 'the hair disaster', and how much worse it could have been, they headed to the bar.

'Ali?'

She recognised the voice immediately, and turned to look to her right. 'Hello, Simon. Oh hi, John. Is Sasha here?'

John shook his head. 'She's at yoga.'

'I love what you've done with your hair,' Simon said, staring at her as if she were a complete stranger. 'Why the sudden change? You never mentioned wanting to colour your hair.'

'I don't tell you everything, Simon. Just like you keep things from me. But thanks. Everyone seems to like it. Especially my new boss.' Why she said that last part was a mystery. It just popped out.

Jules gave her a curious look but was wise enough not to say anything.

'You can join us if you want,' Simon said, his brows furrowed as if thoughts were running around his head like balls on a billiard table.

'Thanks. But Jules and I have things to discuss. Private things. I'm sure you understand.'

'Not really. But fine. You know where we are.'

'I hear Maggie is off on a cruise. That was a surprise.' Ali watched clouds flit across Simon's eyes.

'It was to me, too. I'm really pleased though. It's about time she got on with her own life.'

'Yes. Well, you've clearly been getting on with yours.'

'What does that mean?'

'You figure it out, Simon. You're the intelligent one, not me. Lovely to see you. But now I need a drink.'

She turned her back on him and leant her elbows on the bar. Shivers ran up her spine and her heart matched the pace of her breathing. Was this anger? Was it adrenaline? Or was it because she was sure another barrier had formed between her and one of her best friends?

Chapter Eleven

Ali didn't want to wait for Bruce to arrive. Sitting in The Golden Dragon, a mere few metres from Simon, was making her feel sick. She wanted to have it out with him. To ask why he had lied. About the house, the inheritance. Everything. But what was the point? He could easily lie again.

She finished her drink and smiled at Jules. 'If it's OK with you, I think I should go on ahead, and pack a few things. Bruce should be here soon, shouldn't he? And you could always sit with Simon and John. I'm sure you'd be more welcome than me. It'll give me time to tell whichever one of my parents is home tonight, and write a note for the other. No point in telling either of them to pass the message on as they won't speak to each other.'

'Whatever works for you, babe. I can come with you if you want and tell Bruce to meet us there.'

'Thanks. But I think I should be alone when I tell either Mum or Dad. Shall I give you a call when I'm ready?'

'Yep. Sounds like a plan.'

Ali gave Jules a hug and, without looking in Simon's direction, left the pub as quickly as her, still slightly painful feet, would allow. Blisters took longer to heal than she remembered. She wouldn't be dancing in those sandals ever again.

She hadn't been walking for more than a few minutes when the pounding of leather soles on the paving slabs behind her, grew closer.

'Ali, wait.'

Damn. The last thing she needed now was a row in the street with Simon.

'I'm in a hurry, Simon.'

'Yeah. So Jules tells me. You're really moving out? Why didn't you call me? You could've stayed with me.'

He had caught up with her and fallen into step, but she stopped on hearing those words.

'What? In the flat you paid to be converted, in the house you bought from your mum?'

'Why are you looking at me like that? Anyone would think you hated me.'

'I don't hate you. But I am disappointed in you. I thought we were friends. I thought we were close.'

He screwed up his face in confusion. 'Why? We are friends. We are close. What's going on? Have I missed something?'

'You don't get it, do you? You lied to me.'

'When? I … I haven't lied. Not as far as I'm aware. Just tell me what this is about.'

'It's about you buying the house from your mum, and not telling me. About the idea of converting it into flats, being yours, not Maggie's. About you having investments, large enough to pay for all that, and not once mentioning them to me. That's what it's about.'

He blinked several times, as if he didn't understand. 'That's it? That's why you've given me the cold shoulder? Sorry. But didn't you get promoted without bothering to tell me? Haven't you completely changed the way you look without mentioning that you intended to do so? I wasn't lying to you. I simply didn't tell you.'

'That's as good as lying. And, yeah, I should've told you about the promotion. Under normal circumstances, you would've been the first person I called. But that stupid proposal, made me feel … I don't know. Weird. I knew you must be joking. But I wasn't completely sure, and it made me hesitate, I suppose. I was going to call you when I got home, but Jules called and said you were going to the pub, so I thought I'd tell you there. Except you didn't turn up. As for the hair. Jules must have told you she only asked me on Sunday in the pub. The colour was an accident. A mistake. It should've been Strawberry Blonde but it went wrong. But we're talking about hours here, Simon. A day at most. Not keeping something secret for months. Even several years. You've known about your investments all of your life. You knew you were buying the house long before you bought it. Knew about the conversion. But not a word. Not one word. I even asked you if you were sure it was a good idea, because I thought it was Maggie's. You could've told me then that you were buying it from her. That you were the one paying for the conversion.'

Simon shrugged. 'You're right. When you put it like that, I agree. I should've told you. To be honest, I don't know why I didn't. Except that, I thought Mum might feel a bit embarrassed if people in the village found out that her son was buying her house from her. You know how word gets around in a place like this. Mum coming into lots of spare cash might ruffle a few feathers. Now that I'm saying it out loud, I can hear how ridiculous that sounds. But you need to see it from my perspective. Mum's spent her life taking care of me. I wanted to take care of her and I didn't want every Tom, Dick and Harry knowing about it.'

'So I'm just a Tom, Dick or Harry, am I? I wouldn't have told a soul. You should know that.'

He nodded, a deflated look in his eyes. 'Yeah. I suppose I should. What can I say? I'm sorry, Ali. Sorry about everything. About the secrets. About what you see as lies. But mostly, I'm sorry about that bloody, stupid proposal. I don't know why I did that. The only excuse I have is that I was tired and I was drunk. If I could take it back, I would. I do. You're one of my best friends, Ali and I love you. I don't want to lose our friendship over a few stupid words and a few ridiculous secrets. Has any real harm been done? Can't we get past this and still be friends?'

How could she resist that plea? How could she resist him? She wanted to throw her arms around him and cry on his shoulder. But she wouldn't do that.

She shrugged. 'I suppose we can.'

Simon let out a long, deep sigh. 'That's the best thing I've heard all day. D'you mind if I walk with you?'

'Isn't John waiting for you in the pub?'

He smiled. 'Yeah. But I won't be long and besides, he's got Jules for company. After she told us you were moving in with her, and I got up to come after you, she was telling him why she coloured your hair. To match the bridesmaids' dresses, apparently. She'll no doubt be describing them in all their glory.'

A cool wind blew in from the west as he spoke, and with it came a sheet of drizzle. Great. Rain, just when things were beginning to look up.

Then she saw it. Hovering between the slowly setting sun and a cloud of rain – a rainbow. Just a small one, but definitely a rainbow.

She smiled and linked her arm through Simon's. 'I'm sure he'll love that. I don't suppose there's any chance of a piggy back, is there? My feet still hurt from Saturday night, and I continue to blame you for that, you know.'

He raised his brows and beamed at her. 'Jump on. But don't even think about telling me to giddy up because you're not the only one still aching from Saturday night. Oh, and if you get tired of Jules and her wedding planning, Mum goes off on her cruise on Friday morning, so her flat will be free for six weeks, if you need it. I know she wouldn't mind.'

'Six weeks?' Ali hoisted herself up and Simon caught her legs as she wrapped them around his sides. 'I didn't realise she would be away for so long. She really is pushing the boat out, isn't she? Excuse the pun.'

'There were several places she wanted to see and she couldn't make up her mind. Neither could my aunt, so I suggested they go on one that took in as many of the places as possible.'

'In for a penny, in for a pound.'

'Exactly. And speaking of pounds...' He threw her a grin over his shoulder. 'As I said, you're welcome to her flat, but as the owner, I may have to consider charging you rent.'

'Oh yeah? Maggie would give you a clip around the ear if you did. And so would I, you twerp. In fact. Now that I know you're rich, perhaps you should call a cab to take me home. It's a much more glamorous mode of transport than a piggy back.'

'It may be more glamorous, but it's not as much fun. And this is more exclusive. I don't let just anyone climb all over me, you know. Only someone very special is allowed to do that.'

Chapter Twelve

Ali was very glad it was Friday. She had only been living with Jules since Tuesday night and was already considering moving back home. She wasn't sure which was worse: living with her parents and their constant arguing, or with Jules, who was increasingly turning into a first- rate Bridezilla. If this was what arranging a marriage did to a person, Ali was surprised anyone ever made it as far as the aisle.

She could easily return home. Her parents had both been out on Tuesday evening, so she had scribbled each of them a note and left them, in separately addressed envelopes, beside the wooden bowl on the hall table. The notes said the same.

'I'm moving out for a while. I love you both, but I can't stand the way things are. I wish you could remember how much you loved one another, and treat each other with respect. I want you to be happy and I understand that may mean a divorce.

Can't it at least be amicable? I'm staying with Jules. I don't know for how long. Love, Ali.'

Since ten o'clock that night, both her mum and her dad had bombarded her phone with texts and voice messages. Some were apologetic; some simply asked her to return home. She ignored them all, until finally, this morning, she received one text from each which said the same.

'We're going to sort this out as amicably as we can.'

There was no mention of the fact that her dad, who was supposed to have been moving out on Thursday, had done so, or that Alejandro had moved in. No request from her mum to remember that she was having a dinner party that very night at which Ali was expected to be present. Just that one sentence from them both. And that of course, could mean anything.

But there was some sunshine on the horizon. Things were almost back to normal as far as she and Simon were concerned. She hadn't seen him since Tuesday night because today was the last day of term at the Shimmering-on-Sea, River School, which meant they both had rather a lot to do in this final week. Simon would then be able to wind down for the school holidays; whilst Ali was gearing up for the same. But they had texted and phoned each other at least once a day. In addition to that, Bruce was taking Jules away for the weekend, so Ali would have the flat to herself. She would have to work on Saturday but she would have two days of peace, without a hint of some new drama on the wedding front.

But best of all, Aidan Rourke had just walked in to Ali's office.

'Good morning, Ali. Oh wow! What have you done to your hair?'

Instinctively, Ali's hand shot to her head.

'Sorry,' he continued, 'that didn't come out right. What I meant was you've changed the colour of your hair. It looks fabulous.'

Her cheeks were now the same colour, she was sure of that. 'Thank you. Have you come to check up on us? Oh. That didn't come out right either.' She laughed as she got up from her chair. 'How are you? It's lovely to see you again. Have you come to have a proper look around?'

He smiled, and somehow the world looked much brighter.

'In a manner of speaking, yes. It's lovely to see you, too. I'm going to ask two things.' He moved closer to her. 'Make that three. Number one. It's such a glorious day. I'd like to take a kayak out. Will you come with me?'

'Oh. Yes. Absolutely.'

'Excellent. Number two. I came down here on Dad's yacht and I'm planning to stay for the weekend. To get an even better feel for the place. I don't know anyone, apart from you. Will you have dinner with me tonight?'

'Dinner? With you? Tonight?'

He grinned. 'Yes. Unless you have other plans.'

The only plans she had were to go and see a speech therapist as soon as possible. Why did she sound like a gibbering idiot every time she spoke to him?

'No. No other plans. I'd love to have dinner with you. Thank you.'

'Great. What's your address?'

'My address? Oh yes. Um. My parents are going through a separation so I'm staying with my friend at the moment.' As if he needed to know that. She really must pull herself together. 'It's the flat above Shimmering Scissors Hair and Beauty.' She grabbed a piece of paper and a pen and scribbled down the exact address. 'Here. The village isn't particularly large, but it is a bit of a rabbit warren. Unless you know where you're going, it's easy to get lost.'

He took the paper from her and his firm hand brushed against hers. A river of emotion flooded her body.

'Thanks. Shall we say seven?'

Ali nodded. 'Seven? Yes. Seven's great.'

He leant forward as if he was going to kiss her. Instead he whispered: 'I'm really looking forward to it.'

Her ear tingled as his warm breath seeped into it, but a second later, he was walking towards the door.

'Aidan?' She called after him, as soon as she found her voice.

He stopped, turned and his grin spoke volumes. 'Yes, Ali.'

'You said three. You were going to ask me three things.'

'So I did.' He turned away and continued towards the door where he stopped and leant against the frame, crossing his arms and tilting his head to one side. 'It's more of a rhetorical question really. Number three. How do you manage to look so breathtakingly beautiful and so incredibly hot and sexy in a tracksuit, and with your hair tied back?'

Ali's heart pounded in her chest as she met the flash of desire in his eyes.

'Don't answer that now. You can tell me tonight.' He pushed himself away from the door. 'In the meantime, I'll go and get changed out of this suit and into something more appropriate for messing around on a river. I'll meet you downstairs in twenty minutes.'

He was gone. Which was just as well because she couldn't speak if she wanted to.

Shaking, with more than a little desire of her own coursing through her, Ali picked up her phone from her desk and pressed the number for Shimmering Scissors Hair and Beauty. When Jules was working, it was easier to call her via the salon's landline.

'Shimmering Scissors Hair and Beauty,' Daisy trilled. 'How may we make you more beautiful, today?'

Regaining her equilibrium, Ali smiled. She was tempted to say: 'By not mixing up the bottles of hair colour for Jules', but even Jules had admitted that she should have checked the bottles Daisy had put aside for her. Instead, Ali said: 'Hi, Daisy. May I speak to Jules please?'

'Ali? Oh God! I'm so sorry about the mix-up. I got a right bollocking. I deserved it, of course and I'm really, really sorry.'

'No real harm done. Don't worry about it, Daisy. I'm getting to like it more each day. And I'm sure it won't happen again.'

'You can bet on that. I'm lucky I've still got a job. I won't make the same mistake twice. Hold on. I'll get Jules.'

'Hi babe. What's up?' Jules said, a few seconds later.

'If I work through lunch so that I can get away early, is there any chance of a quick wash and blow dry? Aidan has asked me to dinner tonight and I really need to look my best.'

'The demi-god? Tonight?' Jules was beginning to sound like Ali. 'Definitely. We're not leaving until six-thirty and as you know I'm already packed. Can you get here by five?'

'Absolutely. Thanks Jules. But no colour, right? And check that it's shampoo, not bleach, OK?' Ali laughed into the phone.

Jules giggled. 'Got it. No colour. No bleach. Just shampoo and conditioner. I'll check everything twice. See you later, babe.'

'See ya.' Ali ended the call. Now all she had to do was decide what to wear. And find a pair of sandals she could actually walk in.

She collapsed onto her chair and put her feet up on the perpetually open, drawer, leaning her head back and smiling at the large clock on the wall opposite. Eleven o'clock. Only eight hours to go before Aidan picked her up. Then it was anyone's guess what might happen. If the tingles of electricity racing around her body were any indication, she had a pretty good idea. Sexy underwear would definitely be called for, and so would her little black dress. If he thought she looked sexy in a tracksuit, wait until he saw her in that.

She leapt out of her chair, catching her foot in the drawer in her haste and almost falling over. Aidan was waiting for her downstairs. How could she have possibly forgotten that?

Chapter Thirteen

Aidan was feeling rather pleased with himself. Ali was already putty in his hands and he hadn't even begun to turn on the charm. He was a little surprised she was keeping him waiting. He told her twenty minutes and it was already twenty-five. She was probably titivating in front of the mirror in the staff toilet. He had seen the effect his words had on her.

'Sorry. Got held up on the phone.'

Clearly out of breath, she came to a halt, thankfully, before she careered into him. He caught her by the arm. 'Careful. This floor is slippery. I think someone's spilt some water on it.'

She glanced from his hand on her arm to the floor, before meeting his eyes; a curious look in hers. 'Er. That's water from the river. Even the kayaks have a little bit of water in them. It runs down from the paddles.'

She pointed to large white sign on the wall beside him, where bold red letters announced:

'Caution. This is a water sports centre. There will be areas of wet on this floor, despite our best intentions with a mop and bucket. Take care. Broken bones will hamper activities.' Beneath that, there was an illustration of both a man and a woman slipping on separate pools of water.

'At least it isn't sexist,' he said. 'But isn't it a bit light-hearted? Does it meet with health and safety requirements?'

Ali grinned. 'Probably not. But those three do.' She pointed to three even larger signs, positioned strategically so that at least one could be seen no matter where a person was in the vestibule. 'We've got them in the shower rooms, locker rooms, boathouse, lunch area. You name it, we've got one there. We've even got a couple upstairs, and no one should go up there unless they've checked they're as dry as a bone.'

Aidan matched Ali's grin. 'Water in a water sports centre. Who'd have guessed it?'

'Are you ready for this?' she asked, still grinning.

'Oh I'm ready, Ali. And not just for this.'

Clearly flustered, she looked away, tugging at her ponytail as she did so. She obviously hadn't brushed her hair, so maybe her comment about being stuck on the phone was true.

'Um. This way then,' she said, walking towards the door.

Aidan fell into step beside her, close enough to occasionally brush her hand with his, but far

117

enough away so as not to look as if he meant to. Each time he touched her, he could feel her flinch, as if she had received a little electric shock. Oddly, he felt it himself a couple of times. It must be something to do with the floor surface. Certain carpet material produced static electricity. Perhaps this rubber matting did the same.

'Have you done this before?' Ali asked, as they stepped outside onto the wooden dock, where a row of four kayaks bobbed up and down on the glistening water of the Shimmering River.

'No. I'm a virgin.'

Her head shot round, the startled expression, almost comical.

'In a kayak,' he continued, after a few seconds of watching her turn the lovely shade of red he had hoped for. 'In most other areas, I'm an experienced hand.' Another few seconds before adding: 'Like on a yacht, for example. I'm an expert, on a yacht.' The various pauses had the desired effect. He could tell by the way she was avoiding his eyes, she wasn't sure if he was talking about sailing, or sex. 'I'm in your hands. And completely at your mercy.'

Her mouse-like little squeal delighted him. Much more of this and she'd be falling at his feet. Time to be serious.

'Are you OK, Ali? If you're not feeling well, I can ask one of the others to take me.'

She shook her head wildly. 'No. No, don't do that. I'm fine. Just a little nervous. You are my boss, after all. I'd hate to drown you on our first outing.'

Nice recovery. He had to admire her for that.

'I'm a good swimmer. There's no need to worry about me. And I'm sure you'd rescue me, in any event. Or at least throw me a lifeline.'

She nodded. 'But that reminds me. You did sign the waiver form, didn't you? It doesn't absolve us of responsibility, but it's a requirement in case of an insurance claim.'

She was grinning but he wasn't sure whether she was serious or not, although as he had signed the form that one of the team had handed him in the locker room, she was probably serious.

'Signed and as good as sealed.'

'Good. Let's get to it then.' She threw him an incredibly sexy smile. 'Trust me. I'm a professional. I have certificates to prove it.' Unexpectedly, she raised herself on her tiptoes and, leaning towards him, just centimetres below his ear, whispered: 'You're in for the thrill of your life.'

As he watched her saunter towards the river, her long ponytail, a rope of dark red gold glinting in the sunshine, swishing to and fro in time with the sway of her incredibly sexy bottom, a strange feeling swept over him. One he didn't recognise, but instinctively knew meant trouble.

Chapter Fourteen

Ali was having the time of her life. Admittedly, Aidan did come out with some clichéd chat- up lines and innuendos, but playing him at his own game was proving to be rather fun. Judging by some of his reactions, her flirting was having a similar effect on him as his was on her. The more the day went on, the stronger the excitement and anticipation for their dinner date became.

'I suppose we should head back,' Ali said, glancing at her watch, and craning her neck and body to look at him, seated as he was, behind her. 'It's half past twelve. We've covered all the parts of the Shimmering River that are safe for novices and you've seen the lake and the waterfall. You've even battled against this faster section. We wouldn't usually bring people here until they've had at least a couple of days' experience.'

'I have a confession.' He resembled an angelic demon, if such a thing were possible. 'I'm not a complete virgin.'

'I think I grasped that much.'

He leant forward. 'I'd like you to grasp something else.' He grinned as she pulled a face. 'I like a challenge. The thrill of danger is one of the things that excites me. What do you say about tackling the rest of it? I saw the section of rapids from the road on my previous visit. I think I can handle that. Are you up for it?'

She shook her head. 'No. What if something happens to you?'

'I'll be OK. You don't have to worry about me.'

'It's your lawyers I'm worried about, if you drown.'

A burst of laughter filled the air. 'I won't drown, Ali. I'm looking forward to this evening far too much to let that happen. Besides, I've been on wild water before. And on wild women, but that's another story.' He winked and leant back, flicking the tip of his paddle in the river and tossing a spray of water towards her.

She held up her hands. 'Your choice. But I'm not risking my life to save you.'

'I think we both know that's not true. I think we also know the rapids aren't as bad as you suggest. Live a little, Ali. Take a risk.'

'I really should get back. The centre won't run itself, you know.'

'I think you're forgetting I'm the boss. I don't want to pull rank on you or anything, but I'm sure the rest of the staff will understand how important it is for me to get a feel of the place. You're showing me the ropes. Think of this as work, with a little bit of pleasure thrown in.'

'I'd better call and tell them where we are.' She fished around in her pocket and came up empty. 'Damn. I must've left my phone on the desk. We'll have to head back to let them know. We can stop for lunch and then head out again this afternoon.'

'No need.' He pulled his phone from the pocket of his jeans, swiped his finger across the screen, and pressed.

'You've got our number on your phone?'

He nodded and gave her a mischievous grin. 'And I've got your personal number on speed dial.' He held up a finger before she could reply. 'Hi. This is Aidan Rourke. I'm with Ali. She's left her phone on her desk, so I'm calling to tell you we'll be out for most of the day. I've asked her to show me around.' He rang off and slid the phone back in his jeans.

'Did you give whoever it was a chance to speak?'

He shrugged. 'No point. There was nothing for them to say.'

'Do you always get what you want?'

'Yes. Don't you?'

'Very rarely.'

'Well, let's hope we can change that tonight. Is that a diner on the other side of that bridge ahead?'

Ignoring his questionable remark, Ali nodded. 'It's the Shimmering River Diner. It's run by Josie

Tate who's lovely and a brilliant cook, but who unfortunately believes, or would like to, that we're living in 1950s Hollywood, not 2017 in Shimmering-on-Sea.'

'I think that solves the lunch issue. We can pull the kayak onto the bank ahead.'

'Oh can we? Sorry. I'm forgetting. You're the boss.'

She smiled, though a little irritated. He was clearly used to getting his own way. But was that such a bad thing? There was no point in arguing, even if she wanted to. He was the boss.

'I'll pay.'

'You'll have to. I've left my purse in the office too. I don't usually need it on the river.'

He pulled out his wallet and waved it in the air. 'Boy Scout. Always be prepared.'

'Show off.'

They paddled under the arch of the bridge to the bank in front of the diner but before Ali could get out, Aidan beat her to it. He held out his hand and steadied the kayak with the other. She leapt out on her own, making the kayak wobble to and fro in the water.

'Show off,' he threw back at her. Then together they lifted the kayak onto the bank.

'At the top of those stairs, there is a wooden deck. We can sit outside as it's such a beautiful day.'

'After you,' he said.

'No. After you. I insist. You've spent the last hour or so looking at my bottom. I think it's about time I did the same to you.'

He laughed out loud. 'You noticed? Even with your back to me?'

'The seat felt as if it was on fire. Yes. I noticed.'

'You can't blame me for that. It's a very nice bottom.' He walked up the stairs before her.

'And so is yours.'

It was. And not just his bottom. His trim waist, his broad shoulders, and not forgetting his long, sportsman-like legs. The man was a vision, front and back. She could almost picture what he would look like naked.

'Cold?' He was waiting for her at the top of the stairs.

'No. Just a little shiver. I think I'm rather hungry.'

His eyes raked over her. 'You and me both.'

She glanced at her watch. Still so many hours to go before tonight, but she could hardly contain her excitement.

Chapter Fifteen

Simon tidied his desk, took a final look around the classroom and headed into the hall. The last day of term was always frenetic, but it was also fun, and he had the rest of the summer to look forward to. A summer he hoped, that like every year, he would help out, on a voluntary basis, at The Shimmering River and Water Sports Centre. As a local, Maths teacher, all the necessary and enhanced DBS checks had been carried out. Additionally, he held qualifications from the Royal Yachting Association and British Canoeing. Water sports had always been a passion of his. That was something else he and Ali had in common.

Smiling as he exited the two storey, River School building, he pressed the icon for Ali on his phone, and walked towards his home. With one hand, he shrugged off his jacket and rolled up his shirt sleeves whilst waiting for her to answer, revelling in the warmth of the late afternoon sun on his skin.

'Alison Warner's phone.' It wasn't Ali who answered.

'Grace?' Simon asked, recognising her voice. Grace had worked at the centre for years and they knew each other well.

'Simon?'

'Yeah, hi. How are you?'

'Fine, thanks.'

'Great. Um. Is Ali there, please?'

'No, sorry. She's out with the head honcho. Sorry. Aidan Rourke. He wanted a tour of the river and stuff. To see the local sites and what we have to offer, I suppose. From the water, that is. She dashed out without her phone. Aidan called to say they'd be out for most of the day, but his number was withheld, so we couldn't contact him if we wanted to. We do have a number for his next of kin though.' She giggled. 'Sorry. That wasn't funny.'

A knot formed in Simon's stomach. 'How long have they been gone?'

'Ages. They left just after eleven, I think. Maybe a bit later. On her way out, she did tell me she would be working through lunch because she wanted to leave early this evening. If being in a kayak with Aidan Rourke is working, I'll do overtime.'

'*A* kayak? They only took one?'

'Yeah. A two-man kayak. Or in this case one man and a woman. One of the new guys, Ben, who I don't think you've met, told us he overheard

Aidan say he was a virgin. In a kayaking sense. If that's not a come on, I don't know what is. It's a good thing Ali knows how to take care of herself in the man department. I only met the guy today and have spoken to him just a couple of times. Aidan that is, not Ben. I talk to Ben all the time. Can never get the guy to shut up. What was I saying? Oh yeah, Aidan. I don't know him, but I got the distinct feeling he's here for more than just the water sports, if you get my drift. And I don't just mean Ali, either. It's the way he looked around the place. And when he was signing the waiver, I got the impression he wasn't seeing a locker room but something else entirely. Of course, I could be completely wrong. It's just a feeling in my water, as my mum used to say. I'll tell Ali you called, if she ever gets back. That was a joke. Do you want me to give her a message? Simon? Are you still there?'

'I'm here. And I think it's me who's got the message.'

'Sorry?'

'Nothing, Grace. Please just tell Ali I called.'

'Will do. See you soon, I hope.'

'Yeah. Me too.'

Simon rang off and shoved his phone into his trouser pocket. He needed to meet Aidan Rourke, or at least get a good look at the guy. From his conversation with Ali earlier in the week, he knew that she found Aidan attractive. Grace had made it clear she felt the same. For both women, who had completely different taste in men, if their previous boyfriends were anything to go by, to be attracted to him, meant he must be something special. Ali wasn't shallow enough to be interested in Aidan purely for his looks, Simon knew that, but if the guy was good-looking and rich – which Aidan was – he already had two of the qualities a lot of women looked for. Simon needed to know if Aidan was also romantic, kind and had a good sense of humour. If so, Simon might as well kiss goodbye to his hopes of a future with Ali.

He had called to see if she fancied going to The Golden Dragon tonight. Jules and Bruce were going away, and John had told him that he and Sasha were going to John's parents for a curry. But if Ali was planning to leave work early she obviously already had plans. Didn't she say something a few weeks ago about her mum having a dinner party tonight? She must be going to that. That made him feel a little better. At least she wouldn't be seeing Aidan.

He turned into Baker's Lane. He would go for a quick pint in The Golden Dragon now. It was on his route home anyway. Heat radiated through his shirt onto his back as he walked. On second thoughts, he would go to the Shimmering River Diner instead. It was a twenty-minute walk, all uphill from here, but it would be worth it to sit out on the sun-drenched deck and soak up some rays, listening to the gurgling river below. He might as well eat there, too. That would save him cooking anything when he got home. His mum and his aunt were on the way to Southampton, or possibly already there, having both been collected from their respective homes this morning in chauffeur-driven cars, so he didn't have anyone to rush home for.

That was quite a depressing thought. No one at home. Was this what the future entailed? Perhaps he should get himself a dog.

He smiled. His mum only left this morning and already he was feeling lonely. What a prat. But he knew it wasn't really about his mum. It was about Ali. And about realising once again that she may not always play such a significant part in his future.

He tried to concentrate instead on the various fragrances filling his nostrils as he pounded the dusty streets of the village, passing window boxes, courtyards and gardens containing a kaleidoscope of flowers and plants. He recognised geraniums and pelargoniums, roses, poppies and lavender but there were many other delicate blossoms and fragrant plants, the names of which he didn't know. The whirr of lawnmowers heralded the lettuce-like smell of freshly cut grass and the wheat in the fields as he approached, reminded him of breakfast in a bowl with cool, fresh milk.

His mood lifted, he glanced at the stepping stones in the Shimmering River, at the bridge, and back again. Grinning, he skipped lightly across the stones, laughing like a schoolboy when he reached the other side. Several people seated at tables on the wooden deck of the diner applauded him and cheered. He gave a little bow and dashed up the wooden, creaking steps two at a time.

'Well done, Simon.' Tom Warner stood at the top of the stairs, grinning. Simon had to stop himself from falling backwards in his surprise.

'Mr Warner. Hello. I didn't expect to see you here at this time on a Friday.'

Tom ran a hand through his dark brown, silver-grey spattered hair and stood aside to let Simon pass. 'You can call me Tom, Simon, as I believe I have told you repeatedly over the years we've known each other. I've given myself the day off. Several days off, in fact. I've got a few things requiring my attention, as you have no doubt heard.'

Simon nodded. There wasn't much he could say to that.

'It's strange. When we moved out from the house next door to your family, we had no idea it would end like this. We were happy in that house. I often wish we had stayed.'

Again Simon nodded.

'Sorry.' Tom coughed. 'I'm embarrassing you.'

'Not in the least. But I don't know what to say. Is it really over?'

Tom shook his head as if the gesture exhausted him and a strangled laugh escaped through half-open lips. 'Is it ever really over when you love someone?'

Simon didn't respond. He didn't think Tom wanted him to.

'Despite all my years as a divorce lawyer,' Tom continued, 'I've never precisely understood how it's possible to both love someone and hate them at one and the same time. Until now.'

'You mean, your wife?'

Tom squinted. 'Yes, Tabby. Who else could there be? Oh, let me guess. You've heard of my alleged affair with this non-existent woman half my age. Though why would I love and hate her, if she were real?'

'Um. You hate her because she's the cause of your marriage break-up, and love her because, well, because we never seem to be able to pick the women we fall in love with. We just fall in love with them and pray to whoever we believe in, that one day it will all work out.'

Tom eyed him curiously. 'I'm not sure we're still referring to me, are we? Unrequited love, Simon? With Ali, by any chance?'

Simon choked on his foolishness. Ali's dad was the last person he wanted to be aware of his feelings for Ali. Feelings that were clearly becoming more and more difficult to keep hidden.

Tom glanced around them. 'Are you meeting someone here? Do you have plans for the evening?'

Simon shook his head.

'Then I wonder. I'd arrived minutes before you and was planning to while away an hour doing nothing in particular other than eating a meal in the sunshine. How would you feel about me buying you supper? After which, perhaps a stroll to the local pub and a pint or two to drown our respective sorrows. My beloved wife is entertaining, and it seems I'm not invited. Oddly enough, I find that all my male friends either live in London or have sadly passed away. Of course, if you would find it awkward, please don't feel you have to agree.'

'I wouldn't find it awkward in the least. But there's no need for you to pay for supper. We'll go Dutch. I was planning to eat here. I was also planning on having a pint in The Golden Dragon. I'd be more than happy to have company. It seems all my friends, both male and female, are engaged.' He grinned. 'And the only single one being Ali, is I believe, at your wife's dinner party.'

Tom grinned at what he probably thought was Simon's pathetic attempt at a joke. Then a frown formed on his brow.

'Did Ali tell you that's where she would be?'

'Not exactly. But I remember her talking about it a few weeks ago, and I was told she was leaving work early, so I naturally assumed.'

Tom placed his hand on Simon's shoulder as they walked towards a vacant table overlooking the river. 'I hate to be the bearer of bad news, but Ali's not going to be there tonight. She told her mother most emphatically that she had no intention of meeting my replacement, Alejandro, and as he most definitely will be there, I can guarantee, one hundred per cent, Ali will not.'

'Then where …?' He didn't finish the question. He may not know where she was but he was certain he knew who she was with. Aidan sodding Rourke.

Chapter Sixteen

Tabitha Warner looked at her naked reflection in the mirror and grimaced. Staring back at her with red rimmed eyes framed by enough crow's feet to fill a scene from an Alfred Hitchcock movie, was a woman she didn't recognise.

The woman who was once slim with pert breasts and a trim waist, a natural blonde, who, so many people said, was beautiful, had vanished without a trace. In her place stood someone roughly the same height, although perhaps a centimetre or two had also disappeared, or found its way to her now tubby waist – with sagging breasts, and dyed blonde hair to cover the natural grey. Now people lied when they said she was beautiful.

Her husband had been the biggest liar of all. He had told her he still found her beautiful, and yet he had hardly looked her way for some considerable time. Sexy, yet he had stopped touching her months ago. The only person he wanted to spend his life with, yet most of their time they spent apart. Told her he loved her, yet had only said it when she prompted.

It never used to be this way. Not so very long ago she would catch him watching her and smiling lovingly. Would tingle as he brushed past her, or took her hand in his, or wrapped his arms around her, or kissed her and made love to her. Most hours away from work, they had spent together, sometimes just reading, or cooking, or walking, or watching television, but always close.

Now they were never in the same room unless they were arguing. And she couldn't remember the last time he had said the words she longed to hear: 'I love you.' Three words far stronger than bricks, to build bridges. Far more powerful than medicine, to heal wounds. More lavish than the most expensive gift. Three words he wouldn't say unless she asked him, so eventually she stopped asking.

How had things come to this? How had bitterness and hatred replaced happiness and love? Had he stopped loving her before he met the younger woman? Or had he met the woman first and let his love for his wife simply slip away?

What was the point in going over this? She should have asked him many months ago. Instead, she had withdrawn from him, not wanting to be the fool, giving and displaying love and affection where it clearly wasn't wanted. She had found comfort in food. Comfort in wine, too. When she mixed them both together she could almost pretend to be happy.

Attack was the best form of defence. She had learnt that in her early years in law. And she was good at attacking. But others had been caught in the crossfire: her daughter, Ali and her mother, Gertie.

She had said she would try to stop. The truth was she didn't know how. All she really wanted was to love and be loved. Was that too much to ask? Was it too late for love? What she had with Alejandro wasn't love. She knew that. But some wounds need a plaster, however temporary.

And then the final straw. Tom had planned to take the dining furniture. Such a stupid thing. Such an overreaction to replace the furniture with a man. Had she scored points? A tiny victory in a much larger war? It didn't seem so. When Tom was told that Alejandro would be moving in, he hadn't seemed bothered at all. Probably relieved.

'Well,' he said. 'You've always wanted a pet. I hope you don't find that one day he will turn around and bite you.'

Ali was more upset than Tom, so much so that she had moved out. Now seven bedrooms and a study were empty, and so was Tabitha's life.

At least she had made a decision. Tonight, after the dinner party, she would tell Alejandro it was over. He wouldn't be moving in. A short-lived affair. But no one can start a fire without a spark, and a bed can feel just as empty when occupied by two as it can when occupied by one. What was the point in sharing it with someone you didn't love?

Perhaps she should have told Tom he could stay. Made an excuse about it being more financially viable. Would he have fallen for that? But it wasn't wise to pick at wounds. Tom had someone else. She had to face the fact. Someone young. Someone beautiful. Someone he loved.

Perhaps Ali would come home. The house would feel less like a coffin with Ali there.

Ali had changed the colour of her hair. Could Tabitha change the pattern of her life?

She had enough money to retire. She could travel, like she used to. Find new hobbies to occupy her time, instead of other people's sordid divorces. Divorces like her own. Did she want to be in this house when the decree absolute plopped through the letterbox like a dead fish?

She could be in the Bahamas, eating fish. And drinking cocktails. Dancing to a pulsing rhythm, on a hot and steamy night. Relearning how to live. She might still look the same on the outside, but could the inside reflect the woman she once was?

What was the alternative? Divorce, old age and loneliness? She couldn't bear the thought of that. Tom having a wonderful life, while she sat alone in this house, peering out. Absolutely not. She would do anything to avoid that prospect. Anything at all.

What was it her grandfather used to say? 'Change or die.' Yes. That was it.

Taking one last look in the mirror, she turned away. Tabitha Warner had made a decision and she was one hell of a determined woman when she set her mind to it, as well as one hell of a stubborn one.

Chapter Seventeen

'Please don't shout at me,' Ali pleaded, sucking in breath and wiping her damp brow.

Jules tapped the jewel-encrusted face of her gold-strapped watch, with one long, sparkly purple fingernail. 'I thought we said five. Luckily for you, Bruce is also running late. We're not leaving till seven now.'

'So you've still got time?' Ali threw her bag and phone onto the purple sofa beside the reception desk. 'Where's Daisy?'

'Daisy leaves at five-thirty. That was fifteen minutes ago.'

'OK, OK. Don't rub it in.' Ali pointed to her head. 'Strawberry Blonde, remember? Forgive and forget.'

Jules tutted. 'Forgiven, babe.' She tapped her fingers on the back of one of the row of purple chairs in front of the sinks. 'Come and sit. Why are you so late anyway?'

Ali grinned and dashed to the chair, plonking herself in the seat and Jules slipped a purple gown over her clothes.

'I've spent most of the day messing about on the river with none other than Aidan Rourke. And not just on the river. We had lunch at the diner. He was very impressed with Josie.' Ali made herself comfortable. 'But she didn't seem that impressed with him.'

'That's because she's half in love with Simon. No one can compare to him. She probably thinks you're being disloyal.'

'Don't be ridiculous.' Ali laughed. 'She's the same age as his mum.'

'And your point is?'

Ali shrugged. 'Yeah, OK. But I don't think she's in love with him, although she may possibly see him as a surrogate son, or something. I know she was good friends with his dad, long before Sam met and married Maggie. I remember Josie telling me that. We were talking about not realising what we had until it was gone from us, or something, and she started talking about Sam and the fact that they'd been life-long friends. Until he died, of course.'

'Whatever. All I know is that she thinks the sun shines out of his arse. So, what did you and Gorgeous-balls do on the river?'

'Kayaking. We ran the rapids, too. Although they're hardly rapids at the moment. We could do with some prolonged and heavy rain.'

'Oh yes. Just what we need with the school summer holidays starting.'

'Since when have you cared about school holidays? Summer or otherwise.'

'I don't. But I do care about frazzled mothers wanting to get out of the house. What better place to come for a peaceful hour or so than Shimmering Scissors Hair and Beauty?'

Jules washed and conditioned Ali's hair whilst Ali continued to tell her about the day.

'I think Aidan really likes me. Or fancies me at least.'

'Completely understandable, babe.'

'You haven't seen him. He's gorgeous.'

'I have seen him. Google, remember?'

'There're only a couple of photos and they don't do him justice. In the flesh he's even more g-o-r-geous. Anyway. He spent most of the day flirting with me and making inappropriate, but tantalising, sexual innuendos. I'm so excited about tonight, I'm fit to burst'

'Thank you for sharing that image.'

'What? That's nothing compared to what you say to me!'

'Jules! Jules!' The salon door flew open and Sheila Clutterdrew burst in, her face red and contorted with barely suppressed excitement, her arms flapping like a Canada goose before take-off. 'You'll never guess what. You must tell your friend, Ali. Tell everyone. Everyone must know. We've got to stop this. Gather a meeting. Sign a

petition. Do whatever we can. Spread the news.'
She turned back towards the door as if to leave.

'Sheila, babe. What news? You haven't told us. And Ali's here, so you can tell her yourself.'

Ali lifted her head from the sink, waving at Sheila as Jules pointed down at her.

'Ali! Ali! Isn't it dreadful? What can we do to stop it?'

'Er. Still haven't told us, Sheila.' Jules pulled a face at Ali as if to say: 'give us strength.'

'Right. Right. Where to start? It's the water sports centre. A planning application's gone in today. I have it from the horse's mouth.'

Ali's head shot up, spraying an arc of water through the air, droplets of water and conditioner splattering like bullets against the walls. 'A planning application? In connection with the centre? What for?'

'Apartment blocks. Flats. Lots and lots of them. And a few houses. Some of them are even on the floodplain. Everyone knows you shouldn't build houses on a floodplain. Terrible. Must be stopped. Ruin the entire village. Goodness, I'm out of breath. Can I just sit for a minute?'

'Yes, babe. I'll get you some water.'

'Don't suppose there's anything stronger? Such a shock.'

'There's wine. I usually keep a couple of bottles handy.'

'Lovely. Just the thing. But only if one's open.'

'It soon will be. I could do with a drink myself. And I know Ali needs one without even looking at her face.'

Ali glared at Jules and back at Sheila, who wasn't making any sense. 'Sheila. I need to know exactly what you know. Who told you this? Have you seen the application? Who filed it?'

Sheila's head wobbled like a jelly. 'My niece works in the planning department at the Local Authority. She phoned her mum, who's my sister, and told her. My niece saw it with her own eyes.'

'And it's definitely for the centre?'

'Definitely.'

'Who filed it?'

'Some company or other.'

'Connected to the Rourkes?'

Sheila nodded. 'One of their companies. Can't remember the exact name. Definitely one of theirs. They're having a meeting. Oh. Now I come to think on it, I'm not sure she said it was an application. Well it was, but a draft or some such. They want a meeting. Need to discuss possibilities. Options or things. Now what did she say exactly? Let me think. Oh. I'm so flummoxed. Don't know if I'm coming or going.'

Jules handed Sheila a glass of wine and one to Ali before pouring one for herself.

'Take a breath, babe and see if you can recall precisely what was said.'

'God bless you, dear. Just what a body needs.' Sheila took several deep breaths followed by several gulps of wine until the glass was empty.

Ali couldn't wait for her to finish. 'Was it a planning application or was it along the lines of an enquiry? I know that our Local Authority allows people to file a pre-planning application if they wish, to get an indication of the likelihood of permission being granted. I remember Dad talking about it when we first heard the Rourkes had purchased the centre. He told me they could enquire as to likely consent, but at the time, they hadn't. That's still bad, of course and we'll have to do everything we can to oppose it, but it's not quite as bad as an actual application being filed.'

'That's what it was.' Sheila held the glass in the air as if she'd won a trophy. 'They've filed plans and details and paid the fee to have a *pre-application planning meeting*.' Sheila emphasised the words and shook her head. 'Cost a tidy sum, I can tell you. Nothing to the likes of them, but still. Who has money to throw away unless they think there's a chance they'll get what they want? But then some lawyers called and said there'd been a bit of a mix-up. Whatever that means. Wasn't supposed to be submitted for a couple of weeks. Loose ends to tie up. Or loose land, did my sister say? Blowed if I can remember. Loose something. Or lost? Was it lost?' She struggled to her feet, handing Jules her glass. 'Lovely dear. Thank you. Don't understand it all myself. But definitely for the centre. Came to tell you as soon as I heard. Knew you'd pass the news to Ali. No need, as you said because she's here. That's that then. Must run. More people to tell.'

'Sheila?' Ali asked. 'Is that really all you can remember?'

'Afraid so.' She tapped her head. 'These old brains not what they used to be. Where was I off to now? Oh yes. The Golden Dragon. Lots of people there.' Sheila waved as she waddled away in the same frenetic manner she'd arrived.

Ali and Jules watched her depart and then met each other's eyes.

'The bastard!' Ali hissed.

'I'm phoning Bruce. There's no way we're going anywhere tonight.'

'No. Don't do that, Jules. It's Friday night. The planning office is closed. We won't be able to do anything until Monday. Let's think about this. There's a chance, I suppose that Sheila's niece may have got it all wrong, or more likely Sheila, or her sister. I can't believe Aidan would do this. Besides, he spent most of the day with me. And why would he ask me to dinner, knowing that there was an application in the works? Even if they're enquiring about the possibility of planning, that's almost as bad, and he must've known I'd find out.'

'Now, don't blow a fuse.' Jules topped up Ali's glass. 'But you wouldn't have found out if it's just an enquiry. And he wouldn't know that Sheila's niece works there because he doesn't know anything about this village and the people here. Is it possible that he was hoping to hook up with you then disappear into the sunset before you found out? After all, he did make you manager. That meant he didn't have to come to the centre every day and he doesn't have to face the staff when it all hits the fan.'

Ali stared at Jules, shaking her head in disbelief. 'He couldn't. He wouldn't. Oh God. He would, wouldn't he? That explains why he wanted to spend the day with me. To hurry things along. Not waste any time.'

Ali's phone rang from the sofa where she had thrown it.

'Stay there,' Jules said. 'I'll get it. We don't want more water all over the floor.' She handed Ali a towel as she dashed to the sofa to grab the phone only to slip on a tiny puddle of water. Her feet skated beneath her as if on ice and she landed with a resounding thwack on the purple and gold streaked floor.

'Jules!' Ali shouted, hastily wrapping the towel around her head before racing to Jules' side.

'Ow. Ow. Ow.' Jules shrieked.

'Are you hurt?'

Jules moved her legs one at a time, all the while, Ali's phone rang insistently in the background.

'I don't think so.'

'Do you want me to help you up?'

'No, babe. I thought I might just sit here for the night.' Jules scowled at her. 'Of course, I want you to help me up.'

'Sorry. I didn't want to do more damage if you've broken something.'

'Broken something?' Jules squealed.

'It's possible.'

Jules shifted gingerly from side to side, stretched her back, followed by her arms, legs and neck. 'I don't think anything's broken.'

With some effort, and a lot of assistance from Jules, Ali lifted her friend onto a chair.

'You OK?'

'Yeah. Just knocked the wind out of me for a bit. I'll be fine. Pour me another glass of wine, please, babe.'

Ali handed Jules the full glass. 'Are you sure you're OK?'

'Yeah. For once, I'm glad I've got a fat arse.'

Ali giggled. 'One thing you don't have is a fat bottom.'

'Aw, thanks. Are you going to check your phone?'

'Oh. I completely forgot about that.' She grabbed her phone and saw there was a voice message. She retrieved it, stared at Jules and played the message back on speaker.

'Hello, Ali. It's Aidan. There's something I need to tell you. But I'd rather do it face-to-face. I'll see you at seven as arranged. If, by any chance, you hear anything concerning the centre, please

147

ignore it. I'll explain it all when I see you. It's simply a mistake. And thanks for today. It's the best day I've had for a very long time. I'm looking forward to many more like it. Bye for now.'

'The nerve of the guy!' Jules exclaimed.

'Unless it is all a big mistake.'

'Well if it is, he's definitely got some explaining to do.' Jules slowly got to her feet. 'In the meantime, I'm pretty sure I'm OK. We'd better finish your hair, babe before one of us kills ourselves on this floor.'

Chapter Eighteen

Aidan slammed his phone down on the pile of papers on the coffee table. Bloody lawyers. Couldn't they get anything right these days? First, they'd completed the purchase of the water sports centre and entirely missed the fact that the place was potentially landlocked. Without the strip of surrounding land, the only access was from the water. Fine, if you're planning to build a marina; not so good if you're building a housing estate – however upmarket those houses may be. Not all owners would want to shop at Waitrose, via a damn boat.

Now the useless dicks had requested a pre-application planning meeting. He had given them strict instructions that no planning application in any form should be submitted in respect of the centre for at least a fortnight, and only then, on his express say so. Heads would roll for this. It was another cock-up of epic proportions. They'd pay for their negligence, of course, but sometimes there were more important things than money. Did he really just think that? What was wrong with him? Nothing was more important than money.

In theory, even with this error, there was no way Ali, or anyone in the village would find out just yet, but the lawyers had already had a call from some interfering old busy body asking whether it was true that their clients wanted to tear down The Shimmering River and Water Sports Centre. That meant word had somehow got out, despite the fact that the meeting had only been requested to test the lie of the land as far as the planners were concerned. Ali and the others shouldn't have found out about any of it until at least that meeting, and only then, if the planners felt it was particularly controversial – which it would be, no doubt. The Local Authority was in the nearby town of Shimmeringfold, but they'd know the villagers of Shimmering-on-Sea would be against it. If opposition began before the Rourkes had even had the meeting, no amount of 'financial incentives' would help persuade the Local Authority to lean towards the forthcoming application.

This was the last thing he needed right now. Those stupid lawyers still hadn't tied up the loose ends regarding ownership of that adjacent land. They were supposed to have done that first before word leaked out. Now the price of that would go up and the Rourkes may have to haggle. He didn't relish that prospect, and his dad would be furious.

Get in and get out, with as little effort and aggro as possible, that was the family motto – and not just in business, either.

Bugger!

But he knew what these villages and surrounding towns were like. There was always someone who knew someone in the Local Authority planning department, or some bloody do-gooder who had friends in places they shouldn't. Why had he thought this place might be any different? Not that he had. Not really. That's why he'd told the lawyers to delay.

Sodding lawyers. He'd been looking forward to this dinner date with Ali far more than he usually did, and after spending the day with her, he was baying for blood when he found out there was a chance that some twat in the lawyers' office might have screwed it up for him.

He wasn't sure which annoyed him more. The fact that his instructions had been ignored; the fact that the additional land might now cost them a fortune instead of the bargain it, and the centre, were supposed to have been; or the fact that he wanted to see Ali so much that he was prepared to do anything to make that happen.

It shouldn't have to be this hard. It never had been before.

On top of that, the time was going so bloody slowly. The hands on the clock in the stateroom of the yacht must be going backwards before going forwards because every time he looked at them, less than five minutes had passed. And a yacht was no place to pace up and down; it may be spacious for its size, but repeatedly walking around the same area was getting on his nerves.

It was no use. He may as well take the tender ashore and go for a walk along the beach or something. That might help him take his mind off the incompetence of those bloody stupid lawyers, because that was what was annoying him, wasn't it? The fact that they'd screwed up.

Not the fact that Ali might not want to see him and could possibly cancel their date.

Chapter Nineteen

'Tom Warner.' Tom answered his phone after giving Simon an apologetic smile.

'Tom. It's Stephanie. Stephanie Bowls.'

Tom frowned. Why was one of the partners in Tabitha's firm calling him at seven on a Friday evening? 'Hi, Stephanie. This is an unexpected pleasure.'

'I'm afraid it's not, Tom. I was invited to Tabitha's dinner party tonight and, thankfully I arrived early. I rang the bell and got no reply, so I peered through the letterbox and … well, there's no easy way to say this, so I'll simply cut to the chase. There's been an accident. Tabitha was lying at the bottom of the stairs.'

Tom shot to his feet, tipping over his glass in the process.

'I'm on my way. Is she … is she … hurt?'

'Of course she's bloody hurt, Tom. She's fallen down a flight of stairs. At least … I suppose she fell. You two didn't have an argument and—'

'No, we damn well did not! Now is hardly the time to be facetious or cast spurious allegations, Stephanie. You know what I'm asking. Is my wife seriously injured?'

'I'm a lawyer, not a doctor. How the hell do I know?'

Tom gasped in exasperation as he grabbed his jacket and caught Simon's look. 'Tabby's had an accident.'

'Oh God. Is she OK?' Simon stood and grabbed his phone.

'No idea. This bloody woman is no help at all.'

'I heard that, Tom. I called you, didn't I? I'm not at all sure Tabitha would have wanted me to, but I felt you should know. Fortunately, I still had your number from the Bell-Smythe divorce we settled together.'

'What? Stephanie, would you please tell me if Tabby is conscious?'

'No. Well, she wasn't when they bundled her into the ambulance.'

'Ambulance? It's there already? Thank you for calling them, at least.' Tom rushed out of The Golden Dragon with Simon at his heels.

'They were obviously the first call I made. I'm not a moron, Tom.'

'Mind if I come with you?' Simon asked. 'Shall I call Ali? Or would you rather do that?'

'What Simon? Oh, of course I don't mind, and yes, please call Ali. She'll want to know immediately.' He returned his attention to his phone. 'Stephanie? Where did the ambulance take her? The local hospital?'

'St Joseph something or other. Is that the local one?'

Tom sighed. 'Yes. That must mean they don't think it's too serious. The local hospital has limited resources. If they felt she required more extensive treatment, they would have taken her further afield.'

'Good to know. Right. I'll leave it in your hands then, Tom. Got to get an effing train back to London, I suppose, as I obviously won't be getting off with Davidson Throgmorton now, will I? Unless I don't call and tell him the dinner party's off. Now there's an idea.'

'Stephanie!' Tom bit his lip. 'I have more important things to concern myself with than your sex life. Thank you for calling me, and for everything you did for Tabby. Goodbye.'

'Tom! Before you ring off, you may want to know that they had to break in to get to her. I'd call an emergency carpenter and locksmith to come and fix your door, if I were you.'

'I couldn't care less about the door.'

'Tabitha would. And so will your insurers when you are robbed. I suppose I could stay and organise that for you. I could even stay the night in case they can't get here right away. You'll be at the hospital for most of it, I expect. Then I might still have a chance of hooking up with Davidson Throgmorton.'

155

'Stephanie. Please do whatever you think works out well for all of us. I've got to go.' He rang off, shoved his phone in his pocket and glowered at Simon who was matching his frantic pace. 'Lawyers! We're a bloody heartless bunch, sometimes. Have you spoken to Ali?'

Simon shook his head, his phone at his ear. 'No answer. I've left a message for her to call either you or me. I'm calling Jules right now, to see if she knows where Ali is.'

'Good thinking. I'll get us a cab. Best not take our cars as we've both been drinking. The last thing we need is to be pulled over by the police. Then I'll call the hospital and see if there's any news. Perhaps I should do that first?'

'No, Tom. Cab first. That way we'll be headed to the hospital without more delay.'

'You're right. I don't appear to be thinking terribly logically tonight. Oh, and that reminds me.' He pressed the number for the local cab company from the contacts list on his phone. 'I'd better call Gertie and pick her up on the way. There'll be hell to pay if we go to the hospital without her.'

'Call two cabs. You go to the hospital. I'll go and get Gertie.'

'It's a good thing you're here, Simon.'

Simon smiled compassionately, his phone still at his ear. 'Jules? Finally. Thank God. Listen, I need to get hold of Ali. Do you know where she is? Her mum has had an accident. Tom, Gertie and

I are on our way to the hospital but Ali isn't answering her phone.'

Chapter Twenty

Aidan held out a bouquet of twenty-four red roses tied with a lavish red and gold heart-patterned, bow.

Ali glanced at the flowers dismissively before glowering at his contrite face. 'You've got some explaining to do, and it'll take more than flowers, however beautiful, to placate me at the moment, or to persuade me to go out to dinner with you.'

Strands of his dark hair lifted in the gentle, summer-evening breeze and he ran a hand through the short fringe to push it from his face. 'You've heard then?'

'Yes, I've heard. So it's true?'

He shook his head. 'Not exactly. May I come in and explain?'

'No. What does, "not exactly" mean? Is there a planning application or isn't there?'

'Yes and no. Wait!' He slapped his free hand against the front door as Ali began to close it. 'It wasn't a planning application. It was an application for a pre-planning meeting, just to see whether there was any likelihood of planning being granted in the future. Nothing is definite. We simply wanted to keep our options open. The centre is only just managing to keep afloat – excuse the pun – and as businessmen, we need to explore all alternatives available to us. It was just an idea. An idea that I pulled the plug on, shortly after I met you. It wasn't supposed to have been filed. It should have been shelved. The lawyers cocked up.'

Ali stared at him. Was he telling the truth? The part about the centre not being profitable was true. 'I know Denny Davis, the former owner was struggling to keep his head above water.' Rats. Now she was using puns. She took a deep breath. 'Are you actually saying that you were going to lodge redevelopment plans for the centre but you met me and suddenly and miraculously changed your mind? Do you honestly expect me to believe that I had such a dramatic effect on you, you were willing to scrap an elaborate plan with the potential to make you and your father's companies millions of pounds?'

'No. I'm saying we were going to make enquiries regarding the future likelihood of permission being granted, should we decide the centre wasn't viable. The meeting was merely to see what may or may not be possible. But at this moment in time, I don't expect you to believe anything I say. I'm just telling it like it is. And without wanting to bruise your ego in any way, shape or form, it wasn't just you that made me change my mind. It was seeing the centre again. I'd only seen it once, very briefly before we bought it, but coming back, made me view it in a different light. I told them to put it on hold on Monday. After spending such a fabulous day with you today, I called them this afternoon to tell them I'd made a decision. That's when I found out they'd screwed up and filed it. Believe me, I was livid. I'm rather ashamed to say, I completely lost it, and I think someone may end up paying for their incompetence with their job, in addition to the compensation we'll be getting for the firm's negligence.'

He didn't look ashamed. If anything, he looked angry but also a little … smug.

'Their job? You mean someone might be sacked over this?'

'Undoubtedly.'

'But that's awful. Everyone makes mistakes, Aidan. No one's died. I agree that perhaps someone should be hauled over the coals for it, but losing their job is a bit drastic.'

An odd expression appeared on Aidan's face, but it disappeared in a flash. It was as if he had suddenly realised he'd said the wrong thing and was trying to make amends.

'Oh I agree. It may not come to that. I'll see if a word or two from me will have any effect. We do give the firm a substantial amount of business, in spite of their recent screw ups, so you never know. It may do something.'

'That's a kind thought.'

'Hey. A man's got to do what he can to put things right. Is there anything I can do to put tonight, right?' He grinned and cocked his head to one side. 'At least take the flowers, even if all you do is throw them at me.'

Ali smiled. 'They are beautiful flowers. It would be a shame to throw them at you.' She reached out and took the bouquet. 'Thank you.'

He stepped awkwardly from foot to foot. 'Um. I'll leave you in peace then. I really am sorry, Ali. You'll never know how much I was looking forward to tonight. I can't quite believe it myself, so why should you? I hope, in time, you'll see that I mean what I say.' He hesitated for a moment, threw her a rather pathetic smile and turned to walk away. 'Goodnight, Ali. I hope you have a better evening than I know I'll be having.'

'Aidan, wait.' Was she really going to say this? Did she honestly still want to go out on this date? 'I'm not sure whether I should believe you or not. It sounds a little far-fetched and it's definitely confusing. But I believe in people getting second chances. So I'll go to dinner with you tonight. Assuming you still want me to, of course.'

His face lit up like a street lamp. 'Still want you to? You have no idea how much I want you. You'll have a good time. I can promise you that.'

'Come in then. I'll put these beautiful flowers in water and grab my bag.'

He followed her up the stairs leading to Jules' flat above the Shimmering Scissors Hair and Beauty salon, and waited whilst Ali tried to find a vase amongst the chaos.

'Excuse the mess,' she said. 'Jules is planning her wedding and she believes in exploring everything on offer, hence all the magazines, swatches, samples, books, DVDs and boxes.'

'Really? My place looks just like this, and I'm not planning a wedding. Well. Not yet, anyway. But who knows what the not too distant future may bring?'

Ali shot a look at him. That was a throwaway line; it must have been.

'Can I help?' He added.

'Thanks. I've only been staying here for a few days, so I'm not sure where Jules keeps her vases and she and Bruce left for a weekend away, less than five minutes ago, so I don't want to call her and ask. Oh wait. I think I've found one.' She pulled out a tall, cut glass vase, and smiled at Aidan. 'Purple. I might have guessed. Jules has a thing for purple and gold.'

Aidan cast his eyes around the room and grinned. 'I'd never have guessed.'

'You should see her salon downstairs. And don't even get me started on the wedding invitations, bridesmaids' dresses, table decorations, floral arrangements, buttonholes and wedding cake.'

Ali took the vase into the kitchen to fill it with water and Aidan followed her, leaning against the door frame and watching her every move. At least, it felt as if he was.

She placed the roses in the vase and arranged them as best she could with shaking hands. The intensity of his gaze disconcerted her. As if she stood in a spotlight on an otherwise empty stage, performing the role of her life to win a much-desired part.

She turned the tap on again, letting cold water trickle through her fingers and over her palms. She added soap, in the pretence of washing her hands, not just trying to cool her overheated body and then quickly dried them.

'Jules has even planned her wedding so that it falls during Advent,' she continued, rambling in order to avoid his eyes. She grabbed the rose-filled vase and placed it, like a make-shift shield, in front of her as she walked towards the doorway. 'Apparently, purple vestments are worn in December. Although the local vicar very kindly told her that he would wear whatever colour she wanted, if it meant that much to her. Provided she agreed to attend church more frequently than she currently does. Which means she only has to go a couple of times in future because until now, she never goes at all. Other than on Christmas Eve.' Aidan hadn't cleared her path so she had no choice but to stop in front of him, push past him, or ask him to move. 'We all … go to church … on Christmas Eve … for some reason.'

Without a word, he took the vase from her, placed it on the purple painted cupboard to one side of the door and slipped his arms around her waist.

'Oh,' was all she could manage.

He grinned, and it was the sexiest grin she had ever seen.

'I didn't know that.' His face was merely centimetres from hers, his voice soft and sensual. 'About Advent and purple. But I do know this. Something's happened to me since I met you. The first time I saw you, you took my breath away. Tonight …' His increasingly passionate gaze wandered from her face to the glimpse of her breasts in the low-cut, black dress she was wearing, and back again. 'You've done more than take my breath away. I think you've also taken my heart.'

'Aidan,' she croaked. 'I …' Her voice trailed off as his lips came down on hers in a kiss that was gentle but at the same time, demanding and possessive.

She steadied herself by grasping the kitchen worktop beside her with her right hand, her legs seemingly buckling beneath her. For a split second she considered pushing him away and raised her left hand to do so but clung to his arm instead, her fingers twisting the cloth of his jacket the more she leant into him. She rose herself up, in the low-heeled sandals she had borrowed from Jules, until she was on tip-toe and hungrily returned his kiss. All thoughts of planning applications, lies and the future, gone in what was undoubtedly a moment of madness, but somehow, she didn't care.

Every move of his hands, every brush of his mouth against her skin, sent new sensations racing through her. She tugged at the sleeves of his jacket, sucking in a breath as his fingers unzipped the side of her dress; moaning his name when his hand slipped inside, and cupped her bra-less breast. She heard him whisper her name, his voice cracking with emotion and he kissed her again, deeper this time, more demanding, more passionate. His hand slid down, hitching up the hem of the short dress and pulling her closer. His fingers moving oh so slowly towards the slash of black lace she wore beneath.

'Ali!'

That sounded like Jules was calling her in the distance. Why on earth was she hearing Jules' voice at a time like this? Guilt? A warning voice in her head? It definitely couldn't be Jules in person. She and Bruce left for their weekend away about five minutes before Aidan arrived.

'Ali! What the …!'

The living room door banged against the wall, and Jules stood in the doorway, eyes bulging, mouth wide open.

Chapter Twenty-One

Gertie shuffled along the corridor towards the waiting room, and Tom stopped pacing when he saw her and Simon.

'Where is she? Where's my Tabby-cat? Is she badly hurt?'

Tom was almost grateful for the company, even if it did mean tolerating Gertie's odd conversational manner. At least Simon's conversation would make sense.

'I'm waiting for the doctor to tell me. He's examining her now.'

'So she's alive? Thank the Lord for small mercies. What's taking them so long?'

'The ambulance no doubt only arrived here shortly before I did. They need time to ascertain what injuries may have resulted from her fall.'

'I'm sure she'll be fine, Gertie,' Simon said. 'She's in good hands. Let's sit down and wait.'

'Simon's right,' Tom said. 'There's nothing we can do but sit and wait.' Tom had always liked

Simon, but tonight the young man had risen significantly in his estimation. Simon had proved to be a man of logical thinking; someone a person could turn to in the midst of chaos.

'You sit and wait, if you like. I'm going to find someone to give me some answers.'

'Let her go,' Tom told Simon, with an affectionate smile. 'She's like her daughter. There's no point in trying to stop either of them doing something when they've set their minds on it. Believe me. I have learnt that the hard way. Did you manage to contact Ali? I've been trying since I got here but there's no reply.'

'No. But I did get hold of Jules who told me she had left Ali at her flat less than five minutes earlier. She got her boyfriend, Bruce to turn the car around immediately so that they could go back to see if Ali was still there. Apparently, Ali has a date tonight.'

'A date? Ali? With whom?'

'Aidan Rourke. Jules said he was picking Ali up at seven.'

Tom glanced at his watch. 'So they may have left for their date before Jules gets there?'

Simon shrugged. 'Possibly, but I hope not. Jules has no idea where he was taking her, so until Ali eventually picks up her phone, we have no way to get in touch with her. I don't know anyone who would have Aidan Rourke's phone number.'

'No. Nor do I.'

Simon sat; Tom resumed pacing, and watched as Gertie grabbed the first man she saw wearing a white coat.

'Are you a doctor, young man?'

Clearly surprised to be grabbed so firmly on the forearm by a frail old woman, half his size, the doctor took a step back, blinking as he did so.

'Cat got your tongue?' Gertie persisted.

'I'm sorry, madam, but would you mind letting go of my arm, please? And yes, I am a doctor. I'll call a nurse to help you.'

'I don't want a nurse. I want to know where my daughter, Tabitha Warner is and if she's injured or not. You should know if you're a doctor. And if you don't know, young man, then I suggest you find out. Pretty damn smartish, too. Unless you want to find out just how strong a frail old woman can be when she's worried sick about her only child.'

'Please forgive her doctor,' Tom said, marching towards them. It was clearly time for him to intervene. 'But I'm sure you can understand how anxious we are for news. Tabitha, who is my wife and is also the daughter of this, usually pleasant, well-mannered woman, had an accident tonight. We weren't present, so have no idea as to the extent of her injuries. We appreciate how busy you all are, but if there is any way that someone, anyone, can set our minds at rest, we would be exceptionally grateful.'

Gertie burst into tears the second Tom had finished and whether it was Tom's words, or Gertie's tears, the doctor seemed to mellow.

'I completely understand. I'm not sure if there's anything I can do but I'll see if I can find someone to help you. What did you say the patient's name is?'

'Tabitha Warner. Mrs Tabitha Warner,' Tom said, the words scratching at his throat. 'My wife.' He wouldn't have reason to say that for very much longer if the separation and divorce went ahead.

'Please give me a few minutes. If you will kindly go back to the waiting room I'll see what I can do.'

Gertie hesitated but Tom grabbed her arm and ushered her back the way they had come, saying: 'Thank you, doctor. We greatly appreciate it.'

Chapter Twenty-Two

'Jules!' Ali tugged at her hem as Aidan abruptly released her. He smoothed back his hair and coughed; she pulled up the zip at the side of her dress. 'Did you forget something?'

'No. But I think you did. You hardly know this guy. That's not important now. Where's your phone? Why aren't you answering it?'

'What? I don't know. In my bag, I suppose.'

'Then check your bloody messages! Both Simon and your dad have been trying to get hold of you for the last fifteen minutes or so. Sorry, babe.' Jules shook her head and dashed towards Ali. 'I didn't mean to shout at you. That's the last thing you need.' Elbowing Aidan out of her way, she grabbed Ali in her arms and hugged her. 'Your mum's had an accident.'

'What!' Ali pushed herself away from Jules. 'When? How? Is she badly hurt?'

Jules grabbed Ali's hand. 'I don't know, babe. All Simon said was that she was found at the bottom of the stairs by someone, and that the person called an ambulance.'

'Oh my God! Where is she?' She darted a look at Aidan who seemed uncertain what to do. 'I must go to her.'

'Of course,' Aidan said.

'We'll take you,' Jules offered. 'Bruce is in the car outside. Your mum was taken to St Joseph's.'

Ali dashed to the sofa and searched her bag for her phone, but couldn't find it. She tossed the bag to one side and frantically moved books, swatches, cushions and more as she hunted for the phone. 'I can't find my phone! Where's my phone? Where is it?'

'Don't panic, babe,' Jules said, helping her to look. 'We'll find it. And I'm sure your mum will be fine. It'll take a lot more than a flight of stairs to do her any serious damage.'

'I'll go with you, if you like,' Aidan said, stepping forward and squeezing Ali's arm as he assisted in the search. He looked at Jules. 'Aren't you and your boyfriend supposed to be going away for the weekend?'

Jules narrowed her eyes at him. 'How do you know that?'

He threw her a friendly smile. 'Ali told me.'

'Oh. Yes we were. But obviously we won't be now.'

'Oh, you must, Jules,' Ali said, abandoning her search. 'As you said, I'm sure mum will be fine, and even if she's ... well, she will be perfectly OK, so we won't think about anything else. Whatever the situation is, there really isn't much you can do. Dad and Simon must be at the hospital, and probably Gertie too. Oh sod the phone. Let's just go. Wait! I can hear it.' She turned back and saw Aidan holding his phone in his hand.

'I'm calling you to help you find it.'

'Why didn't I think of that?'

Her ringtone was coming from the vicinity of the sofa but it couldn't be there; they'd already searched that.

Aidan got down on his knees and felt beneath. 'Got it.' Retrieving it from where it had fallen, he handed it to Ali, switching off his own phone as he did so.

'Thank you,' she said, staring down into his eyes. Um. If you wouldn't mind coming with me, just for an extra bit of support. That would be really kind of you.'

'I'll go anywhere you want me to, Ali. You only have to ask.'

'Jesus.' Jules rolled her eyes, grabbed Ali by the arm and led her towards the door. 'I don't care what you say. Bruce and I will at least take you to the hospital. If we get there and your mum is absolutely fine, then – and only then – will I even consider leaving you.' She shot a look at Aidan. 'Come on then, if you're coming. And grab Ali's bag from the sofa. She may need it.'

Chapter Twenty-Three

'I have some news,' the young doctor declared, keeping a safe distance between himself and Gertie, and directing his words to Tom. 'Good news, I should add. Mrs Warner is conscious, rational and vocal and doesn't seem to have suffered anything more than a few bruises.'

'Thank the Lord for that,' Gertie said, sniffing. 'Are you sure?'

The doctor nodded. 'Yes. There don't appear to be any broken bones, and as everything seems to be working as it should be, without excessive pain, we're not intending to send her for x-rays. We're keeping her in overnight for observation but all being well, she should be able to go home tomorrow.'

'That is good news,' Tom said, smiling broadly.

'She can remember falling, quite clearly,' the doctor added. 'She's certain that she was within a few steps of the bottom, so the fall wasn't as great as first suspected. Landing on a hardwood floor is what rendered her unconscious. We'll obviously keep an eye on her in case of concussion, but there are no signs of that at the moment.'

'May we see her?' Tom asked.

'Yes. She's in Bennett Ward. That's just along the corridor, one floor up. Take the lift to the first floor, turn right and it's the third set of double doors on the left. She's in a private room. I believe it's room two, but the nurse on the ward will confirm that.'

Gertie scuttled forward and grabbed the doctor's hand, visibly startling him. 'Thank you so much, young man. You seem to be as wise as an owl. Now that wasn't difficult, was it? Simon? Would you mind waiting until Ali-ba-ba gets here? She'll need to know where to find her mum.'

'Of course. Jules texted to say they were on their way. They should be here any minute.'

'Come along, Tom. Don't just stand there like a statue.'

Tom rolled his eyes. 'I'm not … Oh never mind. I'm coming, Gertie. Thank you so much, doctor.'

'You're welcome.' The doctor gave Tom a brief smile, threw Gertie a wary look, nodded his head and marched away.

'Dad!' Ali raced towards them as Tom turned back to meet her. 'How's Mum? Have you heard? Is she OK? She's not badly hurt, is she?'

Tom caught her in his arms, hugging her as tightly as he could without stopping her from breathing. 'A doctor has just told us that she's fine. No broken bones, merely a few bruises. She can return home tomorrow, all being well.'

Gertie had remained where she was, but she stretched out her arms, and when Tom finally released his daughter, Ali ran to her gran and they hugged too.

'Hello, Jules,' Tom said. 'And Bruce. Thank you for finding Ali and bringing her here.'

'Our pleasure, Mr Warner,' Bruce and Jules replied, simultaneously.

'Oh Jules,' said Ali, smiling at her friend before running back to her and giving both Jules and Bruce a hug. 'You two get off on your wonderful weekend. There's no need to hang around here. Thanks for everything. I'll text you and let you know once I've seen Mum.'

Jules seemed a little uncertain but Tom met her eyes and smiled reassuringly. Jules smiled back before giving Ali another hug.

'Well, if you're sure, babe. Give her our love. We'll chat later, OK? Bye then everyone.'

'You must be Aidan,' Tom said, spotting the tall, strapping young man hanging a few metres back as Jules and Bruce left. He was staring at Ali as if he couldn't take his focus off her. 'I'm Tom Warner, Ali's dad.'

Aidan stepped forward, giving Simon a passing smile as he reached for Tom's outstretched hand.

'Hello, Tom. Yes, I'm Aidan. Aidan Rourke. Very pleased to meet you, although I wish it had been in better circumstances. I'm so glad to hear that Mrs Warner's OK and hasn't suffered any serious injuries.'

'Yes, we all are. Pleased to meet you, Aidan. We were on our way to see Ali's mum. Would you like to join us, or will you stay here?'

'I'd love to say a quick hello, if it's not an imposition.'

'Not at all. Simon is joining us, aren't you Simon?'

'Absolutely,' Simon replied, frowning slightly at Aidan.

'Well come along then,' Gertie said, linking her arm through Ali's the moment Ali returned to her side.

Tom felt a sharp slap on his arm as the five of them proceeded along the corridor, their shoes squeaking on the hospital floor.

'What was that for, Gertie?'

'You, being as foolish as a goldfish. Don't you think there's something we need to discuss?'

'Discuss? Please enlighten me.'

'The doctor said Tabby-cat can go home tomorrow.'

'Yes, I heard him. That's wonderful.'

'Is it? Go home to what? An empty house? Ali's moved out. You've moved out. Who's going to look after her? I'm too old to be running up and down stairs with cups of tea and plates of toast.'

176

'I'll move back in, of course,' Ali said. 'Unless …? Um. Where is Alejandro, by the way? Was he there when Mum fell?'

'Alejandro?' Tom repeated. 'I'd completely forgotten about the man. Stephanie didn't mention him, so possibly not.'

'Well … did he move in, or didn't he?' Ali glanced from Tom to Gertie.

'Don't ask me, my angel. Tabby-cat never tells me anything these days. But if I know my daughter at all, I'd say that was a definite no.'

Tom shook his head. 'I don't know. We'll have to ask your mother.'

'I bet he didn't,' said Gertie. 'So, Tom, you'll have to move back in, too. Ali can't keep a twenty-four hour watch on my daughter, and Tabby needs to be watched in case of concussion. It sometimes pops up days later, you know. You're still her husband. Act like it.'

'I'm perfectly happy to move back in, if that's what Tabby wants. But I think we had better ask her before we start altering her new living arrangements. The last thing we need is for her to lose her temper.'

Gertie chuckled. 'Or you may be the one at the bottom of the stairs, is that what's worrying you, Tom?'

'No, Gertie. That is not what's worrying me. My wife having a seizure brought on by high blood pressure is what's worrying me.'

'OK,' Ali said. 'Let's just see what Mum wants, shall we? And, let's all try not to argue in the process.'

Chapter Twenty-Four

'Mum.' Ali rushed to the bedside and gently wrapped her arms around Tabitha as she opened her eyes.

'Ali? Darling! How did you know I was here?'

'Stephanie called me,' Tom said, hovering in the doorway.

'Tom? What are you doing here?' Tabitha's face flushed.

'We're all visiting you, Tabby-cat,' Gertie said, shuffling into the room.

'Mum?' Tabitha croaked.

'Well, she knows who we all are,' said Gertie, sitting on the chair beside her daughter's bed, on the opposite side from Ali. 'That's a good sign.'

Tabitha glanced around the room. Her head felt as if an upside-down porcupine had landed on it and her face ached from ear to ear. She could see her right cheek bulging slightly beneath her eye and it appeared to be turning purple.

Simon stepped out from behind Tom's shadow. 'Hello, Mrs Warner. I'm so pleased you're OK. We were all very worried there for a moment.'

'Simon? You're here too. Yes. I expect some of you were.' Her gaze settled on Tom, but he didn't rise to the bait. He simply smiled. A smile that lit up his eyes, not just his face. Tabitha quickly looked away. 'And who is that?'

Aidan stepped into the room. 'Hello, Tabitha. May I call you Tabitha? I'm Aidan Rourke. Ali and I were on a date tonight when Jules told us the news. I hope you don't mind me tagging along. I just wanted to make sure everything was OK. I'm so very pleased you didn't do any serious damage to yourself.'

Tabitha shot a look at Simon, then Ali, to Gertie and Tom and finally back to Aidan. 'On a date, you say? Well, I sincerely apologise for ruining it. It's good to meet you, Aidan, and no, I don't mind you tagging along at all. If Ali wants you here, you're most welcome.' She smiled down at her daughter, whose face was resting against her shoulder. 'I'm sorry, darling. I'm fine, as you can see. Why don't you and Aidan continue where you left off?'

Ali's face flushed crimson and she lowered her eyes. 'No. We're fine here.'

'There's no rush,' Aidan said, with a bright smile. 'We can continue our date another time.'

'Honestly.' Tabitha shifted slightly in her bed. 'I'm fine. It was merely a silly accident. I caught one of the heels of my sandals on the edge of the stair, couldn't regain my balance, and went head over heels. I was more than halfway down though, so it wasn't as bad as it could have been.'

'You need carpet on your floors,' Gertie said, glowering at her.

'Oh heavens!' Tabitha's eyes opened wide. 'My dinner party! My guests. Do they know?'

'I believe Stephanie was dealing with that,' Tom said, 'so there's no need to worry. She is also dealing with organising someone to repair the door. She may have to stay the night, and I told her that she could. I hope that's all right with you.'

'Door? What door? Did I hit a door?'

Tom laughed. 'No. Thank goodness. Just the floor. The emergency services hit the door. They had to break in, in order to get to you.'

'Oh. Yes of course. And yes, if Stephanie wants to stay at the house I don't have a problem with that. Besides, it's still half yours.'

'Which brings us nicely to something we need to discuss,' Gertie said. 'You can come home tomorrow, but clearly you'll need looking after. Ali's offered to move back in, and of course I'll come and help out, but I can't leave Bertie and Bonnie. So Tom's agreed to move back in, too, and before you start one of your tantrums, Tabby-cat, it makes perfect sense. For once in your life, do what's best for all of us.'

Tabitha met Tom's eyes. 'Are you sure it won't be too much of an inconvenience?' For the first

181

time in several months, she made sure there wasn't a hint of sarcasm in her voice.

'I'm happy to do it. It's not an inconvenience at all.' Tom smiled and moved closer to the bed.

'It'll only be for a day or two, I suppose.' She was still holding his gaze.

'I expect so. But one can never be too careful with these things. Let's just play it by ear, shall we?'

'That's a good idea. Thank you, Tom.'

'There's no need to thank me. You're my wife. It's the very least I can do. I have to tell you, Tabby. I've never been so panic-stricken in my life as I was on receiving Stephanie's call. It's a good thing I was with Simon. He was able to remain cool and calm, whilst I was quite the contrary.'

'You were?'

'I was.'

'Well,' Gertie said, getting to her feet. 'There's clearly nothing much wrong with you that a little privacy wouldn't cure.' She kissed Tabitha on the cheek. 'I love you, my darling. Don't go throwing yourself down any more stairs.'

'Oh? You're leaving? Thanks Mum. I love you too. And I promise I'll be more careful in future.'

'Ali,' Gertie added. 'I think you and your young man, and Simon and I, should leave your mum to rest. Come along.'

Ali hesitated but Tabitha smiled and nodded. 'I'm fine, darling. I'll see you tomorrow.'

'OK. But call me if you need anything. I love you, Mum,' Ali said, kissing Tabitha and giving her another hug. 'I'll see you tomorrow, and I'll move back in, in the morning. I've got a day off tomorrow.'

'I think you should take a few days off,' Aidan suggested. 'I'm sure the centre will be able to cope without you for a short time. We'll discuss it later this evening. Good night, Tabitha. I hope to see you again soon.'

'Thank you,' Ali said, walking towards the door. 'See you tomorrow then, Mum.'

'Thank you all for coming.' Tabitha raised her hand and gave a gentle wave, all the while staring at Tom.

'Are you sure you're all right?' Tom asked. 'Do you need anything? I can stay if you would like me to.'

'Of course you're going to stay,' Gertie said, ushering Simon, Aidan and Ali towards the door. 'We're the ones who are leaving. Simon, close the door behind us. Private rooms should be just that. Private.'

Chapter Twenty-Five

Ali linked her arm through Gertie's. 'Well, you're a dark horse. Are you trying to get Mum and Dad back together?'

Gertie smiled and patted Ali's hand. 'I'm not doing anything, my angel. I just think that sometimes people need a shock to remind them of what is important. Your parents have had a shock. What they do with that is entirely up to them. So Simon?' She glanced in his direction. 'How do you feel about taking an old woman for a rum and black in The Golden Dragon?'

'I don't know about taking an old woman,' he said, with a grin. 'But I'm more than happy to take you.'

Gertie chuckled. 'Your tongue's as smooth as silk, my boy.'

'May we join you?' Ali asked, half-laughing, half-blushing. Aidan's tongue had been as smooth as silk, but not in the way Gertie was referring to Simon's.

'The more the merrier.' Gertie threw Aidan a curious look. 'Have you been to The Golden Dragon, young man?'

'No. But I'm sure it's delightful.' He didn't sound delighted.

'Oh it is,' Simon said, a coolness in his tone that wasn't there a moment ago. 'Quite delightful. And it's our favourite pub. But then, it is the only pub in the village, so it would have to be.'

Ali glanced at Aidan. 'You don't mind if we postpone our dinner date, do you? I know my mum's OK, but it's all been a bit of a shock and I'm not sure I'm ...' Ali let her voice trail off. She could hardly say she wasn't in the mood for sex, in front of Simon and her gran.

'Not quite in the right mood, you mean.' Aidan finished the sentence for her. 'I understand, and it's really not a problem. I don't mind at all.'

His tone belied his words. He sounded as if he minded rather a lot and the smile he gave her was like those given by campaigning politicians, or TV celebrities trying to sell the public something. Ali wasn't at all convinced – but for some reason, she wasn't sure she really cared.

Chapter Twenty-Six

'Are you going to sit down?' Tabitha asked Tom, smiling over at him as he stood in front of the closed door. 'Unless you want to go, of course. I know my mother put you on the spot. Please don't feel you have to stay if you don't want to. I'm fine, Tom. Truly I am. And it was an accident you know. I didn't throw myself down the stairs or anything.'

Tom gave her a curious look. 'I didn't think for one moment that you had. What on earth made you say that?' Tabitha shook her head, and Tom continued: 'As to Gertie putting me on the spot, if I minded, that wouldn't have mattered. I'm here because I want to be here, not because your mother told me to stay.' He walked over to the chair beside her bed, and sat, leaning back into the seat.

Tabitha fiddled with the off-white bedspread. 'I'm glad you're here.'

'As am I.'

'Life's been pretty hellish for the past few months, hasn't it?'

Tom shrugged. 'It's been a little difficult. For both of us. For all of us. Ali clearly hasn't been having much fun being stuck in the middle.'

'How did we get to this? When did you stop loving me? Was it something I did? Or did you just meet *her* and fall in love?'

He frowned and shifted in his seat. 'Firstly, Tabby, I have never stopped loving you. Secondly – and before I say this, let me just remind you that for a moment tonight I thought you might be dead – so I'm telling you the truth. I swear to you on everything I hold dear, there is no other woman. There never has been and there probably never will be. I don't know why you think there is.'

Tabitha hung her head and bit her bottom lip. 'I saw you with her, Tom. More than once. I … I followed you. You were having dinner on one occasion, on another, having lunch.'

Tom's mouth fell open. 'You followed me? When? Where? Why?'

'Because you started drifting away from me. I could tell. And you suddenly seemed to be working late more often. I … I know the signs. I hear about such things on a daily basis. I wanted to know if you were seeing someone else.'

Tom shook his head. 'I have lunch and dinner with several women, Tabby. And you know I didn't mean that in the way it sounded. I have lunch with colleagues, dinner with friends. I've

187

even had lunch with Stephanie, on more than one occasion. We were on opposing sides in a rather messy divorce. It doesn't mean anything. I'm not sleeping with any of them. I don't want to sleep with any of them.'

'This was different. When I saw you together you seemed so happy. You … you held her hand across the table. She's gorgeous. About twenty-five and has the reddest hair I've ever seen.'

Tom frowned then suddenly burst out laughing. 'Oh, Tabby. That's Alice. My god-daughter, Alice Clarke. I told you she was visiting London from the States and that I'd met her a couple of times. I even asked you if you wanted to join us, but you can't abide her parents and you didn't want to come in case you said something out of place, remember?'

'Alice? It can't be. This woman was absolutely beautiful. Alice is still a girl … isn't she?'

'She's a young woman. A very beautiful young woman, I agree – but I'm not in the least bit attracted to my god-daughter, I can assure you. And I can tell you exactly why I was holding her hand. Squeezing it reassuringly, to be precise. She's fallen head over heels in love with one of the solicitors in my office and she was intending to ask him out, but was nervous about doing so. I squeezed her hand and told her she had absolutely nothing to be nervous about. I then told her the story of how you and I met – and that it was you who had asked me out. That's why I was so happy. I was talking about you and how we fell in love.'

'It was really, Alice?'

Tom nodded. 'Yes. Believe me, Tabby. The only woman I've ever wanted to sleep with was you. It still is you. Unfortunately, it seems some time ago, you decided you no longer wanted to sleep with me. You cringed every time I tried to touch you. You sneered every time I paid you a compliment. I think the question should be when did you stop loving me? Not, when did I stop loving you?'

'I … I have never stopped loving you, Tom. Ever. But I knew you didn't really want to sleep with me. Didn't want to touch me, or hold me, or kiss me. How could you? I mean look at me. I'm not the pretty young thing you married. I'm almost sixty. I've got wrinkles on my wrinkles. Everything's sagging. How could you possibly want me?'

Tom reached out his hand and took one of hers in his. 'Is that what you think? That I don't find you attractive? That I don't want to touch you, hold you, kiss you, make mad passionate love to you, like we used to? Because if that *IS* what you think then you are more mistaken than you could possibly imagine. All I see before me, all I've ever seen, is the beautiful, passionate, lovely woman I married. The girl I fell in love with half a lifetime ago. The woman I'm still in love with. You see wrinkles, I see years of laughter, a lifetime of happiness and love. Until the past few months. Then all I saw was that beautiful woman backing away from me. Not wanting me near her. Staying later and later at the office to avoid spending time with me in the evenings. Making plans at the weekends with Ali, or with your mother, or with friends, so that you didn't have to spend the weekends with me.'

'No, Tom! I … I worked late, because you did. I made alternative plans at the weekends because you did. I looked in the mirror and felt unattractive. I was sure you saw the same.'

'Or perhaps we both saw things the other didn't. You saw wrinkles. I didn't. You saw my alleged, other woman. There wasn't one. Only Alice, and friends or colleagues. You thought you were unattractive and backed away. I saw you back away and thought you didn't want me. Instead of us both feeling hurt and rejected by each other, we simply should have sat down together and talked it through. Do you realise we have never done that? Not since things started to go downhill. We went from talking to each other and loving one another, to avoiding each other and giving one another a cold shoulder.'

'And from there we progressed to arguing. Never talking. Just hurting each other even more. Can we come back from this? Do we still have a chance? I love you, Tom. I've never loved anyone else.'

Tabitha darted a look towards the door as it opened, and Tom turned his head to see who was there.

A tall, slim, olive skinned man in his late fifties stood in the doorway. 'Mi Amor,' he said, holding out a single red rose and smiling passionately at Tabitha.

'Alejandro!' Tabitha screeched.

'Alejandro,' Tom said, through clenched teeth.

Chapter Twenty-Seven

Tom's head was pounding like a steel drum at a Caribbean party and, as he struggled out of bed in his sister's guest bedroom, he cursed himself for drinking so much. He had had a few beers with Simon at The Golden Dragon before he'd got the call from Stephanie, followed by sharing several bottles of his sister's best Burgundy, not forgetting almost an entire bottle of his brother-in-law's 30-year-old single malt whisky. It was a wonder he wasn't comatose and a miracle that he could stand – albeit somewhat shakily.

But it wasn't only the excessive amounts of alcohol still flowing around his system that was making his head hurt. It was also the knowledge that his hopes and dreams had crashed and burnt just moments after it had looked as if his future would be heavenly.

Why had he lost his temper so badly at the hospital yesterday? Why had Alejandro's sudden appearance made such a difference? Why hadn't he let Tabitha explain, as she was clearly trying to, instead of storming out like a teenager having a hissy fit? Did the fact that his wife had had a brief affair really change the way he felt about her? The irony of it all. Tabby had accused him of cheating, yet he was completely innocent. He had never suspected she might be frolicking in bed with some sleazy-looking Spaniard, until Tabby had informed him earlier in the week, that the Spaniard would be moving in the minute he moved out.

The shock of Tabby's accident had, absurdly, made him forget that little fact. Until Alejandro had arrived with a red rose in his hand and flowery words in his mouth. And the worst part of all was that Alejandro didn't look in the least bit sleazy. Unfortunately, he looked a lot like George Clooney.

Tom wasn't sure he could compete with that, despite Tabby saying that she had never stopped loving him. She obviously loved them both. Was it simply more convenient to reconcile with him? She could still see Alejandro on the side.

Perhaps too much water had flowed beneath their bridge. Perhaps reconciliation was just a piece of flotsam in a stormy sea; something to cling to before all hope was lost.

Someone knocking on the door, sounded like a barrage of cannon fire, and his niece, Sasha bringing an insipid cup of coffee at eight-thirty in the morning, and informing him that she was on her way to pick up Ali and to take her home, was hardly the best start to his day.

'Thank you. Please get out,' he said.

'Good morning to you too,' Sasha replied. 'The headache pills are in the bathroom cabinet. I'll tell Ali you may be a while.'

'Tell Ali I won't be coming. No don't. I'll go to the house and talk to her myself.'

'Whatever. You look like death you know.'

'Thank you, Sasha. So will you if you remain here very much longer.'

Sasha laughed, and just to add insult to injury, slammed the door on her way out.

Chapter Twenty-Eight

Ali awoke in bed in Jules' spare room, unable to quite believe how much had happened in a single day. A day spent flirting had led to her almost having sex with a man she hardly knew – and wasn't completely sure she trusted. Her best friend had caught them just in time. Her mum could easily have died, but thankfully hadn't. And if last night was anything to go by, Aidan and Simon would clearly never be friends. She was rather grateful when Gertie had insisted on them all getting a cab together, from The Golden Dragon, and dropping Ali off first as both Aidan and Simon seemed to be in competition over who should walk her home. What was it with men and this need to be a protector? She was perfectly capable of walking home, especially, as she had had to remind them both, she was staying at Jules' just a few doors away. Even the cab driver laughed when they told him the first stop was at the Shimmering

Scissors Hair and Beauty salon, but Gertie had insisted, so everyone went along with it.

Besides, as she had informed Aidan and reminded Simon, Simmering-on-Sea was hardly the sort of place where a person would feel unsafe walking the streets, no matter what time of day or night. The last serious crime here – so bad it made the local paper – was when a juicy piece of roast beef was stolen from Susan Tilliman, the village florist's kitchen table. She had left her door open and the thief had sneaked in and out, within seconds. Fortunately, the criminal, who was known for such thefts, was apprehended and a photo appeared in the paper, but as the culprit had four legs and a tail and went by the name of Baddog, no formal charges were made. Baddog's owner, Perriman Day, son of the village butcher, replaced Susan's joint of beef with a much larger one, and a romance was born. Their wedding photo was front page news beneath the words: 'Local Couple Meat and Marry'. No one in the village was sure if that was merely a typo, or a feeble attempt at an amusing headline.

Ali turned over in her bed and hugged her pillow to her. By far the best thing that had happened yesterday – surpassing even Aidan's wonderful kisses – was that there seemed to be a chance her mum and dad might be getting back together.

It just goes to show, miracles do happen, and that sometimes – only rarely, mind you – love really does last forever.

With that thought in mind, she pushed her pillow aside, leapt out of bed and dashed into the shower. She was moving back home today, and although last night both Aidan and Simon had offered to help, she had phoned Sasha and asked if she would help, instead. It was only a few cases, after all. She and Sasha could manage those without the help of men. For some reason, Ali didn't want Aidan or Simon around today. Seeing them together last night had made her feel oddly uncomfortable. And if the looks they had thrown one another had been spears, both men would be dead from their wounds and lying in pools of blood, instead of sitting and scowling at one another whilst downing pints of beer.

But she wasn't going to dwell on them today. She was moving home. Her dad was moving home and her mum was coming home from the hospital. The Warner family home might be exactly that once more – the home of the happy and loving Warner family.

It didn't take long to pack her things, and by the time Sasha arrived at nine o'clock, Ali had brought the cases downstairs and was sitting on the largest, waiting by the front door.

'Blimey, Ali. You're keen. How long have you been sitting there?' Sasha asked, jumping out of the car and opening the boot.

'Not long.' Ali handed her a couple of cases and grabbed the other two herself. 'It's such a lovely morning, I didn't want to waste a second. May we stop off at Susan's Bloomers on the way? I want to get some flowers to make the house smell wonderfully welcoming. What flowers do they have in Thailand? I suppose they're mainly tropical ones. I wonder if Susan will have any. I'd like to bring some of the heady fragrance that surrounded Mum and Dad on their honeymoon. I told you last night, they might be getting back together.'

Ali climbed into the passenger seat and Sasha started the engine of her Nissan QashQai and drove towards the Warner house.

'Yeah. About that.'

Ali swivelled in her seat to look at her cousin. 'What? That sounded ominous. Do you know something I don't?'

Sasha nodded. 'I'm afraid so. Uncle Tom came around to ours last night after he left the hospital and he and Mum had rather a lot to drink. I didn't hear it all because every time I walked into the kitchen, Mum pointed at the door and said: 'Brother and sister con flab. Leave.' So I didn't have much choice.'

'But you stood at the door and eavesdropped, didn't you?'

Sasha threw Ali look. 'Of course I did. I heard your dad say that the conversation had been progressing exceptionally well and that, unless he was very much mistaken, there was a distinct possibility of a reconciliation ... Why does he do that by the way? Always talk as though he's in court or something?'

Ali shrugged. 'He's a lawyer. What can I say? Get on with it. It all sounds exceedingly promising so far.'

Sasha tutted. 'Don't you start. Anyway, and then he said: 'It appears that Tabby and I have been proceeding with our lives under a rather large misapprehension. We still love one another. Unfortunately, we had failed to make each other aware of that fact.' Sasha shook her head. 'You see. It's a good thing I've got such a fab memory. Any normal person would have said something like: it was all a misunderstanding and we still love one another.'

'For heaven's sake, Sasha. Please stop criticising my dad's speech pattern, and tell me why you seem to think there may be a problem.'

'OK grumpy knickers. I don't think there's a problem. I know there is. And it's called, Alejandro.'

'Alejandro!' Ali's mouth fell open just as Sasha pulled up outside the house. 'What's Alejandro got to do with anything?'

Sasha shrugged as she stepped out of the car. 'Don't ask me. Dad came home, saw me eavesdropping and told me off. I'm sure he thinks I'm still twelve sometimes, instead of thirty-three. He joined Mum and Uncle Tom in the kitchen, and sat on the chair facing the door, so he could see me if I hung around.'

'So that was it?'

Sasha lifted the cases from the boot 'No. But all I know for sure is that Alejandro turned up at the hospital after the rest of you had left and your dad wasn't at all happy about it. I think I heard him say that they had a row and he stormed out. Your dad that is, not Alejandro. But it was difficult to hear exactly what was said because I was leaning over the banister on the stairs and trying not to be seen by Dad. Which obviously failed. He got up and shut the kitchen door and suggested the three of them go and sit in the conservatory. Anyone would think they were having top secret negotiations, not discussing Uncle Tom and Aunt Tabitha's love life.'

They walked in silence towards the front door and just as Ali was about to put her key in the lock, she remembered. 'Bugger! We forgot to stop and get the flowers.'

Sasha pulled a face. 'Judging by the mood your dad was in last night and again this morning when I took him coffee, it'll take a lot more than flowers to sort this out.'

'My key doesn't work!' Ali's skin prickled as an icy river ran through her. 'Oh my God, Sasha. Either Mum is already home and has changed the locks. Or Dad has. It's started already.'

Sasha shook her head and rang the doorbell. 'I wonder about you sometimes. Even I remember being told that the emergency services had to break in, and your mum's friend was staying the night so that the door could be repaired and the lock could be replaced.'

Ali breathed a sigh of relief. 'Oh yes. I'd completely forgotten. That's one less thing to worry about.'

Chapter Twenty-Nine

The first row of the day started early, although it wasn't so much a row as a complete and utter shock. And it didn't involve Tabitha and Tom; it involved Ali, Stephanie and a naked middle-aged man.

'Oh good heavens,' Stephanie exclaimed, answering the door, wearing nothing but a man's white, silk shirt. 'What time is it?'

'A little after nine,' Ali said, stepping inside. 'It's good to see you again, Stephanie. It's been a long time.'

'And you, Ali. My goodness. You've changed the colour of your hair. Wasn't it always blonde? What made you decide on … whatever colour that is? Not that it doesn't suit you. It's just … well, so different … and unlike any colour I've seen before.'

'Thank you. Change does us all good sometimes.'

'Indeed. And hello, Sasha. It is you, isn't it? I rarely forget a face. You're Tom's niece. We met at one of Tabitha and Tom's garden parties.'

'Yes. At a barbecue three years ago, I believe,' Sasha said, rolling her eyes at Ali the moment Stephanie's back was turned.

'I'll nip upstairs and get showered and dressed,' Stephanie said, already on her way.

'Thank you for staying,' Ali said. 'And for the door and everything.'

'It was my pleasure. The new keys are in that heart-shaped wooden bowl. Three sets. I settled the carpenter's and locksmith's bills. The invoices are there on the hall table. Tell Tom he can settle up with me any time.'

She dashed upstairs, leaving Ali and Sasha to follow slowly behind, on their way to returning Ali's belongings to her room.

'Why did Stephanie just go into your room?' Sasha asked, as they neared the top of the stairs.

'Did she?' Ali increased her pace and marched along the hall. The door to her room was ajar and she pushed it open, horrified to see that not only was Stephanie now naked in Ali's ensuite shower room, but that there was an equally naked man in Ali's bed. And it definitely wasn't Aidan.

'Who the hell are you?' Ali shrieked, her cases landing on the hardwood floor with a resounding thud.

'Davidson Throgmorton,' the man declared, sitting bolt upright and displaying more of himself than either Ali or Sasha wanted to see. 'Who the hell are you?'

'Alison Warner. You're in my bed!'

Davidson's face turned the colour of the white sheet, barely covering him; all that bedding would be going to a charity shop after Ali had thrown it in the washing machine.

'I had no idea.' He scrambled to his feet, attempting to wrap the sheet around him. 'Please accept my apologies. I came to attend Tabitha's dinner party but when I arrived, Stephanie told me what had happened. I stayed to be of assistance to her.'

'Mission accomplished,' Sasha said, grinning from ear to ear.

Davidson glanced towards the ensuite shower where Stephanie was completely oblivious of the man's predicament. 'Perhaps I might ask you if I may quickly use your shower and then I shall dress and leave immediately.'

'Why not?' Ali said, with a sigh. 'You've clearly used everything else. Help yourself. And don't rush off on my account. I suppose technically, you're a guest of my mum's. She would expect me to offer you breakfast, or coffee at the very least.'

Davidson looked as if he had tied the sheet too tightly; his face contorted into a pained expression. 'That's most kind of you. But one doesn't wish to overstay one's welcome and I have suddenly remembered, I need to return to London in somewhat of a hurry. Thank you for your exceptionally kind offer.' He pointed lamely towards the shower. 'I'll just join Stephanie. No. What I meant was … To shower. Not to …' He coughed loudly and turned away. 'If you'll excuse me, ladies.' He strode manfully to the ensuite, dragging the sheet behind him like an ill-fitting toga, and closed the door behind him.

Sasha burst out laughing and Ali scowled at her.

'Oh come on,' Sasha said. 'You've got to see the funny side of this.'

'It's my bedroom, Sasha. That's my bed. And that's my shower. I'm struggling to see anything funny about it at the moment. I'm going to use another room. I may have to have this one fumigated.'

Sasha's continued laughter followed Ali along the hall, but the doorbell chiming for all it was worth caused both of them to stop in their tracks.

'That might be Dad,' Ali said, excitedly.

'Doubtful. Unless those headache pills work miracles. It might be your mum. Although I suppose the hospital will insist on someone picking her up. Is anyone doing that? Because I'm sure it won't be your dad.'

'I don't know,' Ali said, dumping her cases and heading back towards the stairs. 'I assumed Dad would be. I'll have to find out. Whoever that is at the door is certainly insistent.'

'It's probably Gertie,' Sasha said. 'You know how much she hates waiting.'

Sasha was right.

'Good morning, my angel. I hope you've got the coffee on. I think I had one too many rum and blacks last night. Is Tom here yet?'

Ali kissed her gran on the cheek and stepped aside to let her in. 'No to both, unfortunately. But I'll make some coffee now and then I'll phone Dad and find out what's happening. According to Sasha, the reconciliation may be in tatters.'

'What?' Gertie was clearly surprised. 'Sasha? Tell me everything.'

Sasha repeated what she had told Ali, whilst Ali made coffee and several slices of toast.

'Well that's not good,' Gertie said when Sasha had finished. 'I'll have to get my thinking cap on. Ali-ba-ba? Why are you making so much toast?'

'Oh you haven't heard the best bit,' Sasha said, laughing. 'There was a naked man in Ali's bed this morning.'

'Not that Aidan chap?' Gertie said, frowning. 'He may be as bright and shiny as a new penny, but I've a feeling that Simon's worth a pound compared to him.'

'Why?' Ali queried. 'I thought you liked him.'

'I didn't say I didn't. I just don't like him as much as I like Simon. So who was the naked man?'

A cough at the doorway heralded Davidson's presence. He had Stephanie by his side. 'That would be me, unfortunately.'

Gertie turned in her chair and looked him up and down, nodding as she did so. 'I wouldn't object to finding him naked in my bed,' she said to Ali. 'You young girls are so difficult to please.'

Davidson turned the colour of Ali's red mug, as Stephanie possessively took his arm.

'Sorry about the confusion in the bedroom department,' she said. 'I thought it was a guest room. The couple of drawers and one of the wardrobes I looked in, were empty. It has such a lovely view, which was why I picked it. Not that I saw much of the view in any event. Anyway. No harm done, I hope. We'd better dash. Trains to London on a Saturday leave a lot to be desired.'

'I've made toast,' Ali said, staring at the pile heaped before her.

'That's very kind,' Stephanie said, stepping backwards. 'But I don't eat wheat, and it's much later than I realised. Hugs and kisses to Tabitha. Tell her I'll be in touch.'

'Goodbye and thank you,' Davidson said, still blushing.

Sasha burst out laughing yet again.

'What's so funny this time?' Ali asked, grabbing a slice of toast and slathering it with butter.

Gertie chuckled too. 'Didn't you notice, my angel? That poor man's flies were still undone. I

207

don't think he'll forget today in a hurry, but he clearly got dressed in one.'

Chapter Thirty

The second row of the day was definitely a row, as was the third. Ali tried to prevent the second, and had hoped to avoid the third, even though instinctively she knew that was wishful thinking.

Sasha had long gone and Gertie was snoring softly on one of the large, comfy white sofas, having eaten several rounds of toast and drunk two full pots of tea. Ali had been trying, unsuccessfully to reach her dad on the phone. Someone needed to pick up her mum and if her dad wouldn't do it, Ali would have to take a cab and collect her mum herself.

'Finally!' Ali said, when her dad answered his phone after her eighth attempt. 'I've been calling you for almost an hour and have already left seven messages. Why haven't you returned my calls?'

'Please don't shout, darling. I believe my head may explode. I couldn't find my phone and have only just discovered it in a fuchsia bush in your aunt's garden.'

'I've been calling her too. No one answered.'

'No. I believe my sister and brother-in-law are feeling somewhat hungover this morning. We all had rather too much alcohol and are suffering for our sins. I fear I shall be no use to man or beast today.'

'And what about mum? Someone needs to bring her home. Dad? Are you still there?'

'Yes. As I said. No use to man or beast. Perhaps Alejandro could play the part of the knight in shining armour. I am certain it is a role the man would relish.'

'What happened last night?'

'I got exceedingly drunk.'

'I meant before that, Dad. What happened at the hospital after we all left?'

'Enlightenment.'

'Dad? Are you still drunk?'

'I believe that is a distinct possibility.'

'So explain the enlightenment.'

'It seems I am a fool. I love your mother. She says she loves me. But she's sharing her bed with a Spaniard. Not that I have anything against Spaniards, you understand. Or any Europeans. Brexit or not. But when they resemble George Clooney, bring roses and romance, it is a little difficult to like them, especially when they're sleeping with one's wife.'

Ali was losing her patience. 'But you already knew about Alejandro, Dad. And despite what Mum said, he definitely hasn't moved in, so it can't all be roses and romance, can it? Perhaps Mum had second thoughts. Perhaps she realised she still has feelings for you.'

'I believe she does. Perhaps it was the Spaniard who had second thoughts? Have you thought about that? I've thought about little else? And that's a lot of thinking.'

'I can't have this conversation with you, Dad. You're not making any sense at all. You don't even sound as you normally do. I suggest you take a shower, drink several cups of coffee, have some breakfast and then come around here and sort this out. Because, do you know what, Dad? I am not prepared to go through all the arguing again. I'll get a cab and collect Mum myself.'

A few seconds after she rang off, her phone rang again, and she answered it without looking, assuming her dad had immediately phoned her back.

'So are you going to get Mum, or not?'

'Um. Yes,' Simon said. 'Of course I'll get your mum, if you want me to, but there's no need to shout at me. Does that mean things didn't work out between her and your dad? I assumed he would be going to get her.'

'Oh God! I'm sorry, Simon. I thought you were my dad. I've just had a row with him on the phone. And in answer to your question, no. Things definitely didn't work out. Alejandro has put a spanner in the works.'

'I'm really sorry, Ali. I know how much it meant to you. But it may not be as bad as you think. There's still a chance. There's always a chance.'

'I don't know. Dad sounded really despondent. Almost as if it's a competition between him and Alejandro, and he believes Alejandro has won. It's as if Dad's given up. As if he is resigned to their fate, and their fate is separation and divorce. Perhaps when he sobers up I'll be able to talk some sense into him.'

'When I was with him yesterday, it was clear that he still loves your mum. I can understand the competition bit, but can't understand him giving up. It's not over until it's over.'

'It feels pretty over to me. But anyway, are you serious about being happy to collect Mum?'

'Absolutely. Are you waiting for her to call, or shall I just go and see if she's ready to come home?'

'Um. Someone's at the door. I'll call the hospital and call you back after that. Hold on a minute.' Ali opened the front door. 'Oh! Oh my goodness.'

'What?' Simon said. 'What's happened? I'm coming over.'

'No! There's no need. And there's no need to go to the hospital. Aidan's here. He's just brought Mum home in a chauffeur-driven limousine.'

'He's what?'

'Brought Mum home. I've got to go, Simon.'

'Yes that's right. Run into his arms. Jesus Christ. I know exactly how your dad feels.'

'What?' Ali watched Aidan help her mum out of the car, whilst the chauffeur, who was obviously the person who rang the doorbell, stood to one side of Ali, holding a massive bouquet of red roses. 'What's that supposed to mean, Simon? Why are you so angry? Aidan's saved you the trouble of picking up Mum. You should be grateful, not annoyed.'

'Yeah right. It's not my gratitude he wants. It's yours. And not just gratitude either. And it seems he's got it. Be careful, Ali. He may not be the man you think he is. I've got a very bad feeling about him. He's hiding something. Once he gets what he wants, he'll be off. I'm pretty sure of that.'

'Don't be ridiculous, Simon. You know nothing about the man. You only met him yesterday, and I have to say you didn't behave like one of my friends should, towards a man I'm dating. And don't tell me what to do. I'm perfectly capable of choosing who to date. I've been doing it for years without your help. Aidan's kind and thoughtful and he doesn't deserve the way you're talking about him. How do you know what he wants? Or whether he'll leave once he gets it?'

'I know he wants you. And I'm also sure he's going to get you. Even if it's just a one- night stand.'

'Simon! That's a horrible thing to say. I've got to go. I'll talk to you when you're in a better mood.'

'You'll have a long wait.'

Simon rang off before she did, and for a second or two, Ali stared at the screen of her phone, displaying the call had ended.

'Hello darling,' Tabitha said, smiling, but not looking particularly happy. Her arm was linked through Aidan's and they walked slowly towards the front door. 'Wasn't it lovely of Aidan to bring me home, and in such style, too? Have you … heard from your father?'

Ali rubbed her forehead and nodded, suddenly exhausted by it all. She walked forward to meet her mum. 'Yes, Mum. It was lovely of Aidan. Dad had quite a lot to drink last night and he's not feeling well this morning, but I'm sure he'll be round later.'

Tabitha reached out and kissed Ali on the cheek. 'I wouldn't count on it, darling. I don't think your father is terribly happy with me. I hope he'll give me a chance to explain.' She gave a little cough. 'But we mustn't bore Aidan with our problems.'

'You couldn't possibly bore me,' Aidan said. Smiling at Ali he added: 'I hope you don't mind me doing this, Ali, but when we spoke half an hour or so ago and you said that there might be a problem, I thought that this might help. And these.' He held out his hand and the chauffeur passed him the bouquet, which he then gave to Ali. 'I assumed you wouldn't have brought the roses from yesterday, so these are a replacement.'

'Thank you.' Ali took the roses in one hand, and linked her other arm through her mum's, placing Tabitha between her and Aidan. 'Thank you for everything. It means a lot to me.'

'If there's anything else I can do, you know you only have to ask. But now, unless there is, I'll leave you to it. The last thing you want whilst you both settle back in, is me getting under your feet. I'll call you later, Ali.'

'Thank you, Aidan,' Tabitha said, whilst Ali merely nodded.

Then they watched him leave in the chauffeur-driven car and Ali had to fight a sudden urge to run after him and ask him to take her away from all this. Away from her mum and dad and the rows. But mostly, away from Simon and his increasingly unpleasant attitude. Anyone would think the man was jealous. Could that explain it? Could Simon be jealous of Aidan?

Chapter Thirty-One

After the shocks and rows of Saturday morning, the rest of the day had passed in a relaxed and surprisingly pleasant fashion. Even Gertie had been loving and supportive to her daughter and when she returned home to her dogs, after lunch, Ali and Tabitha curled up together on the sofa, the French doors to the garden thrown open, and listened to birdsong and soothing background music, whilst Ali read a book to her mum. In the evening, they ordered Chinese and sat and watched TV before Ali helped her mum upstairs to bed and slept in the guest room next door. Ali couldn't remember the last time they had spent so many hours together in blissful contentment. Well, almost blissful and almost content. Ali couldn't let go of the possibility of her parents' now aborted, reconciliation, and she couldn't forget her argument with Simon. She even had a nightmare about it and woke up late on Sunday morning unable to shake off a feeling of dread.

Ali smiled at her mum as Tabitha tucked into a hearty, Sunday morning brunch. Tabitha seemed cheerful again this morning and had stayed in bed until half past ten, which was most unlike her. Tabitha was always up with the larks and went to bed with the owls. Burning the candle at both ends was something she had always done.

Ali had been up since nine. After tossing and turning all night, her mind was still whirling with thoughts of Simon, Aidan, Alejandro and her dad, and sitting on the sofa alone, she hadn't been able to concentrate on her book. Was it too much to ask for things to take a turn for the better?

'Aidan phoned this morning and asked me out to lunch,' Ali said, when her mum had finished eating.

'That's super, darling. You must go. I'll be fine here on my own. That long sleep did me a world of good.' She pushed her plate away and took a mouthful of coffee.

'I am going. But you won't be on your own. There's still a chance you may get dizzy so we're not taking any risks.'

'Is mum coming to relieve you?'

Ali shook her head. 'Dad is.'

The colour drained from Tabitha's face before a flush of pink crept into her cheeks. 'Tom?' Shakily, she placed her coffee cup on the table. 'You've spoken to him? He's agreed to come.'

'Yes. He should be here any minute.'

Tabitha darted a look at her watch. 'But I haven't dressed. Look at me. I'm a complete mess.' She dragged a hand through her blonde hair.

'You look lovely, Mum.'

'No. He mustn't see me like this. I must at least put on some mascara and something a little more flattering than striped pyjamas.'

Ali grabbed her mum's hand. 'They're Dad's pyjamas, and I may be your daughter and far less experienced in these things, but I'm pretty sure he'll find that flattering if not downright sexy. As for mascara, you don't need it, but here.' Ali handed her mum a make-up bag. 'I brought some of your make-up down earlier, just in case.'

Tabitha reached out and kissed her daughter. 'You're an angel, darling.'

Whilst Ali filled the dishwasher, Tabitha applied a small amount of blusher to her cheeks, mascara to her lashes and a smear of the sheerest red lip gloss. She had just enough time to close the zip before the doorbell rang.

'He's here!' Tabitha jumped off her chair and leant against the table, sat back down and tried to look relaxed, stood up again and held on to the back of the chair, finally flopping back onto her seat and resting her forearms on the table.

Ali grinned and went to answer the door, looking back at her mum as she did so. 'Relax, Mum. You look beautiful. The paper is on the table. Pretend to be doing the crossword. Dad always loved to help you with that.'

'I didn't need his help.'

Ali popped her head back round the door. 'I know that and you know that, but Dad doesn't have to. Pretend you do. It may work wonders.'

'How did you get to be so smart on the relationship front?' Tabitha called after her as she walked along the hall.

'I'm not,' Ali called back. 'Just ask Simon.'

Tom was holding a bouquet of red roses when Ali opened the door. He looked nervous – like a teenager on a first date and had clearly made an extra effort with his appearance. He was wearing the trousers and the shirt that Ali knew her mum had bought him almost a year ago, for part of his birthday present. They had still been happy then. Or reasonably so.

'Hello, Dad. Are those for me?'

Tom kissed Ali on the cheek. 'Don't be absurd, darling. They're for your mother. But I expect she already has several from that man.'

Ali stepped aside to let him in. 'I assume you mean Alejandro.'

'Are there others?'

'Now you're the one who's being absurd. There's no one, Dad. No one but you.'

He looked at her in disbelief and blinked several times. 'How ... No one?'

Ali shook her head. 'How do I know? Because Mum told me. And I believe her. And before you ask, she's ended it with Alejandro. Although not because of you. Well, not exactly. She knew she wasn't in love with him. She intended to end it after the dinner party, but falling down the stairs delayed things. She told him at the hospital shortly after you stormed out.'

'She did?'

'She did. She's in the kitchen and she's just had brunch. There's a bottle of champagne in the fridge and I think she may need help with the crossword. I'll come with you to say goodbye and then it's up to you.' Ali linked her arm through his and walked towards the kitchen. 'And do me a favour, Dad. This time, please don't screw it up.'

Chapter Thirty-Two

Tom wasn't completely certain that he had recovered from yesterday's hangover and when Ali had phoned this morning saying that she was going out to lunch and asking if he could come around, he had been tempted to say no. But being forced to do nothing other than lie around in a darkened room drinking copious cups of coffee, had given him even more time than he had been doing of late to consider his future; and he thought he had been doing very little else over the past few months.

He had come to a decision. His marriage was worth fighting for. His wife was worth fighting for. And he would do that, as soon as he recovered from his hangover.

If he had been the one who had had an affair, he would have prayed that Tabby would have been willing to forgive him. Her affair had only started recently and had really been as a consequence of Tabby believing he no longer loved her and that he had found someone else. Surely he could forgive her? Couldn't they try to put all these awful months behind them, and rebuild their lives together? Couldn't he make his wife forget all about Alejandro? It was definitely worth a try.

And now, if what Ali had told him was true, and his daughter had no reason to lie, Tabby had ended the affair on Friday night. There was hope once more and the light at the end of the tunnel was not an approaching train about to run him down, but an opening to a future as bright and sunny as he and Tabby could possibly make it.

Ali said her goodbyes; now he and his wife were alone, and as his daughter had just told him, he mustn't screw this up.

'Good morning, Tabby. How are you?' He smiled at her before he saw what she was wearing, and then the smile grew out of all proportion until his jaw ached from trying not to burst into a bout of blissful, ecstatic laughter. 'Are those my pyjamas?'

Tabby's face flushed crimson as she cast her eyes downwards before looking up again to meet his gaze. 'Yes. Do you mind? They were in the utility room. You left them behind when you … moved out.'

He slowly shook his head. 'Not at all. They look far better on you than they do on me.'

'I don't know about that. I always thought this pair look rather good on you. Or at least, you look good in them. Although to be honest, you look good in anything.' She hesitated as if she had said more than she had meant to. 'Um. Are those beautiful roses for me?'

'Yes,' he said, walking towards her and handing her the bouquet. 'And if we're going to be honest, I also think you look good in anything, but you look particularly good in my pyjamas.'

Tabitha blinked a few times as she took the flowers, and smiled up at him from where she sat. 'It's over between me and Alejandro, Tom. I ended it. I had intended to before the fall. I … I only did it to make you jealous – or to try to, I think. I didn't love him. I meant everything I said to you on Friday at the hospital.'

'And I meant everything I said to you. Before I lost my temper, that is.'

'Is it possible for us to put this all behind us and start again? Can you forgive me for my stupidity? For my lapse in judgement? For my infidelity?'

Tom nodded. 'Anything is possible, and yes, I think so.' He stared into her eyes and she stared into his. 'Ali said you needed help with the crossword. She also said there's a bottle of champagne in the fridge.'

Tabitha smiled. 'I think I may, and I certainly like the thought of champagne.'

Tom took her hand in his and pulled her gently to her feet, entwining their fingers as he did so. 'You know, you do look sensational in my pyjamas. But I have to admit, I think you would look even better wearing nothing, but perfume and that beautiful, incredibly sexy, smile.'

Tabitha opened her mouth to reply but Tom took the words from her with his kiss then he swept her up in his arms and carried her upstairs to the room they had once shared – and hopefully, would soon be sharing again.

Chapter Thirty-Three

It was a perfect, summer Sunday. Looking up from where she sat on the picnic rug Aidan had set out beside the Shimmering River, all Ali could see were miles and miles of baby-blue sky, only interrupted by a few birds, flapping their wings to a rhythmic beat, inaudible from the ground. Occasionally, they caught a thermal and soared higher until the warm air dissipated and they resumed their self-propelled flight. Once or twice, a chalk white slash appeared across the sky behind a tiny, glistening speck as the scorching rays of the golden sun bounced off the fuselage of a plane passing overhead. The cool, clear waters of the river burbled and sparkled, shimmering in the sunlight, casting iridescent droplets into the air and onto the bank.

'I never tire of the beauty of this place,' Ali said, as Aidan passed her a glass of perfectly chilled white wine.

He cast his eyes around and poured himself a glass of red. 'Yes. It's pretty special. More so with you in the scene.'

Ali smiled at him. 'Flattery will get you everywhere.'

His eyes sparkled like the river. 'Really? But that's not flattery, it's a fact. I don't think you realise how beautiful you are. I meant it when I said you took my breath away.'

It wasn't just the sun making Ali's face burn and her skin tingle.

'Are you hungry?' Aidan changed the subject.

'Not at the moment.' She looked into his eyes. She was hungry for him, but she couldn't tell him that.

Slowly, he took her glass from her and placed it with his into the holders in the wicker picnic basket he had brought. He leant towards her and slid an arm around her waist, easing her backwards until she lay beside him on the rug. Without a word, he kissed her; gently at first then harder and more demanding. His other hand caught her long hair between his fingers and twisted it around his hand.

She returned his kiss with equal enthusiasm, her arms wrapping round him and pulling him closer. The rush of the river reverberated in her ears and her temple pulsed as her heart raced. A chorus of birds serenaded them, or so it seemed. Her senses heightened, her blood ran red hot in her veins and every nerve ending exploded with his touch.

He nibbled her ear, her neck and her bottom lip before looking deeply into her eyes.

'I can't believe how much I want you, Ali.' He sounded as if he had swallowed gravel.

'I feel the same about you,' she replied breathlessly.

He kissed her again and there was no denying his passion. Her body responded to his touch and she arched her back as his lips travelled from her mouth to her neck. With one hand, he deftly undid the buttons on the front of her cotton dress and moved his kisses downwards.

She bit her lower lip and screwed her eyes tightly shut as a wave of ecstasy washed over her. If he could have this much of an effect with just a kiss, imagine what else he could do to her. Her head swam with the thought of it as his hand cupped her breast and his mouth moved back to hers.

'I want you now, Ali. Right here. Right this minute.'

'I want you too.'

He smiled and his eyes sparkled with unabashed delight. He reached into the pocket of his jeans and pulled out a small silver packet. He had obviously come prepared. She tried to breathe, but couldn't. Tried to speak, but no words came out. She watched as he unzipped his jeans. Any minute now he would make love to her. And suddenly it was Simon's face she saw, and Simon's words she heard: 'He wants you, Ali, and once he's got you, he will leave.'

It wasn't true. It couldn't be. But did she even care if it was?

'Christ!' Aidan hissed. 'The fucking thing has split. Hold on. I've got another one.'

Ali had no idea why, but suddenly she burst out laughing and unfortunately couldn't stop.

'It's not funny.' Aidan glared at her, swatting away a bee that was buzzing too close for comfort.

'I'm sorry. I don't know what came over me.'

'Well, it wasn't me. I know that much.'

Ali tilted her head to get a better look at him and pushed herself up onto her elbows. 'Don't get mad. These things happen.'

'Not to me they don't.'

'There's a first time for everything.'

'This is our second attempt.'

'Third time lucky, don't they say? Come on, Aidan. Smile.'

He ran a hand through his hair and glanced down at his unzipped jeans. 'Let's go back to my yacht. We'll be more comfortable there. I don't know why I suggested this.'

'A picnic was a wonderful idea. Let's just eat, and enjoy the view for a while.'

'I thought you weren't hungry.'

'I wasn't. But now I seem to have an appetite.'

'And go to the yacht after?'

Ali shook her head. 'I promised Gertie that I'd go around to her house for tea. She's planning a wedding for her dogs and she wants me to help choose their outfits.'

'A wedding? For her dogs? Is she insane?'

'No! And that's not very nice. But I suppose she has always has been a little... out of the ordinary, shall we say.'

'What about afterwards? This evening?'

'You really are keen.' Ali frowned as a thought crossed her mind. 'Or desperate? Why the hurry?'

He looked away and stared at the river. 'I told you. I want you. I can't believe how much.'

'But the moment's gone. So what's the rush? I'm not going anywhere. Are you?'

He glanced back at her, smiled wanly, and returned his attention to the river.

Neither spoke for several seconds, and Ali listened to the sounds of nature; the gurgling river, the birdsong, the buzzing of bees, the soft whistle of the warm breeze.

'Imagine opening the French doors of your bedroom and sitting on your balcony admiring this view,' Aidan said. 'And from your conservatory. And opening the bi-folding doors of your open plan kitchen diner and looking out on all this. Wouldn't that be awesome?'

Ali sat upright. 'No. Because it would spoil the scenery. And certainly not if there were several other houses surrounding it. Aidan? Are you still considering some sort of planning application? Because if you are, then we may have a problem.'

He laughed, but there was no humour in it. 'I think we already have a problem. But no, I'm not considering it. It just suddenly struck me as I sat here looking at this view.'

She reached for the glass of white wine Aidan had taken from her and handed his red wine to him. 'Let's just sit and admire the view for a while.'

'Fine,' he said, turning to swat away another bee, or possibly the same one as earlier, that was hovering above a delicate porcelain bowl containing asparagus spears and softly boiled quail's eggs. 'I hate bees.'

Ali watched in disbelief as the bee banked in flight and flew directly at Aidan's neck.

Chapter Thirty-Four

Gertie couldn't stop laughing when Ali told her about Aidan and the bee.

'It's not funny,' Ali said. 'He didn't tell me he was allergic to bees. He merely said he hated them.'

Gertie held a hand to her shaking chest. 'I suppose you would hate them if a sting from one makes your neck swell up like a melon. I know I shouldn't laugh, but I can't help thinking it couldn't have happened to a nicer man.'

'I don't know what you mean by that. It wasn't just his neck, either. His tongue was swollen, too. And his eyes. I was panic-stricken. If Simon hadn't come along when he did, I don't know what I would've done. Called an ambulance, like he did, I suppose. Aidan should have had his EpiPen with him, but for some reason he'd left it on his yacht. I offered to go with him to the hospital but he called someone on the yacht to meet him there instead. I hope he's OK. He said he'll call me later.'

'Why did Simon come along?' Gertie managed to control herself and threw two small pieces of cake from a strawberry cupcake to her dogs, Bonnie and Bertie, who snaffled up the treats like mini, furry vacuum cleaners. 'Was it by chance?'

Ali frowned. 'Of course it was. You know he volunteers at the centre during the school holidays. He'd taken out a kayak and was checking out the waterways before we get our first big group of kids next week. I should've been working today, but because of Mum's accident, Aidan told the staff that he had given me the weekend off. None of them minded. We all cover for each other if anyone wants to change their shifts. But I still felt guilty when Simon, and Grace who was in another kayak paddling behind him, saw Aidan and me on the riverbank.'

'A fortunate turn of events then.' She tossed two more tiny pieces to her dogs, this time from a lemon cupcake.

'Definitely. Although … Simon and I had a big row on the phone, yesterday and I wasn't sure he had forgiven me. I'm still not sure. He hardly said a word to me and wouldn't even look in my direction.'

'Was the row about Aidan?' She threw another two tiny pieces of cake to Bonnie and Bertie, this time, from a raspberry one.

Ali nodded. 'Yes. Why did you instantly think that?'

Gertie met her eyes. 'It's obvious. Simon's jealous.'

'Of Aidan?'

'Obviously. Who else would he be jealous of?'

'But Simon's just a friend. One of my best friends. I don't think he's jealous. Although I must admit, I did wonder about it. He definitely doesn't like Aidan. I'm really not sure why because he only met him on Friday night.'

Gertie's eyes crinkled into deep small slits as she chuckled. 'You take after your mother, do you know that, Ali-ba-ba? You're both as daft as a brush when it comes to men and love.'

'Why?'

Gertie shook her head and smiled down at her dogs. 'Ah! I think we have a decision about the wedding cake. Raspberry. Definitely raspberry. Did you see the way they gobbled that up?'

'They gobble everything up. Is that what you've been doing? Are all these different cakes, samples for their wedding cake?'

'Yes. They're made from special ingredients so they're perfectly safe for dogs.'

'Safe for dogs! Oh my God, Gertie! Why didn't you tell me? I thought they were for us, for tea.'

'Hmm. I wondered where the orange cupcake had gone. Don't worry, my angel. I'm sure it won't do you any harm. You'll be as right as rain. Now, let's have a look at clothing, shall we? I've seen a pretty little wedding dress for Bonnie and a fetching little tuxedo for Bertie. Bonnie must have a veil and Bertie, a top hat. I'll be as proud as a peacock walking them down the aisle. Why are you pulling that face?'

'Because I think I'm going to be sick. Dog cake, Gertie! Honestly. You really should've told me.'

'Then I should probably tell you not to drink that milk you've just poured from the jug with the picture of the puppies on. It's a special type of goats' milk and it's specifically made for dogs.'

Chapter Thirty-Five

'Simon? Simon, wait.' Ali spotted him as she closed the gate at the end of Gertie's front path. He was striding down the road a few feet ahead of her, and he showed no sign of stopping, despite her calling his name. The low-heeled sandals – the ones she had borrowed from Jules – clattered against the pavement as she ran after him, and pressed on her blisters, which were still in the process of healing. Stopping to take off her shoes, she watched Simon disappear around the corner. 'Simon! How dare you bloody well ignore me.' If he were within range and in sight, she would throw the damn sandals at him. Holding the straps between her fingers and shouting his name yet again, she raced down the road, turned the corner and careered straight into him.

'Was that you calling me?' He steadied both of them with his hands and looked her in the eye.

'No. It was the tooth fairy. Of course it was me, you twerp.'

He frowned. 'If that's your idea of a thank you for saving your new boyfriend's life, you need to buy a book on etiquette.'

'And you need to buy a book to tell you how to stop acting like a jerk. What's got into you lately?'

'I could ask the same of you, but I saw the empty condom packet on the picnic rug, so I think I know the answer.'

'Simon!' Had he really just said that?

'I'm almost grateful to that bee.'

'That's a horrible thing to say. Two horrible things. He could have died from that bee sting, you know. And for your information, the condom packet may have been empty but it hadn't served its purpose. The damn thing split. Don't look so horrified. It split before, not during.'

Simon's frown morphed into a smile. 'You mean you didn't have sex?'

'No, we didn't. And then that damn bee stung him.'

'You may thank that bee one day. It gave its life to save you from being another notch in that man's bedpost.'

'You moron. It did no such thing. If anything, it was an act of revenge. And what do you mean, "another notch"? It's obvious you don't like him, but I don't think Aidan's as bad as you want to believe.'

'Oh really? He's not as good as you want to believe. You do know that he wants to knock down the centre and cover the entire site with luxury flats and executive houses, don't you? Right from the bridge by Josie's diner all the way down to the mouth of the river. Putting aside the fact that it will make you and the rest of the staff at the centre, redundant, it will mean hundreds of overpriced, badly built houses springing up like boils on the scenery. And let's not forget, these so-called homes will all be way out of the price range of any of the locals for miles around.'

'Well, Mr Know it all, that's where you're wrong. Yes, Aidan and his father were looking at options. They are businessmen, after all. But having spent some time here, Aidan reconsidered, and he cancelled all the plans.'

'So that explains why there's going to be a pre-planning application meeting then, does it?'

Ali shook her head. 'The lawyers screwed up. Aidan had given them strict instructions not to file the application. Someone in the office misunderstood and filed it by mistake.'

'Is that what he's saying?'

'Yes. And I believe him.'

'You would. You're besotted with the guy.'

'So what if I am? What's it got to do with you? At least he doesn't shout at me.'

'Not yet.'

'He's besotted with me, too. He can't keep his hands off me.'

Simon glowered at her. 'I can't blame him for that.'

'Oh, don't be so ridiculous, Simon. Anyone would think you're jealous. Your problem is you don't like change. All you're worried about is losing one of your best friends. A shoulder to cry on when your latest love affair goes wrong. Someone to tell your problems to, no matter what time of day or night. I would miss that too. But it doesn't have to be like that.'

'You're wrong. Those aren't the things that worry me. What worries me is losing you, but not in the way you mean. And I am jealous. Jealous as hell.' He shoved his hands into the pockets of his jeans.

Ali hesitated for a moment. 'No you're not. You can't be. We've been friends for more than thirty years and you've never even asked me out.'

'I was worried you'd say no. And I may not have asked you out, but I asked you to marry me, didn't I? And that went down like a lead balloon.' He kicked a loose stone with the toe of his shoe and it clattered along the road as they both stared at it in silence.

'You … You weren't serious,' Ali finally managed.

'I was. You just didn't want to hear it.'

'But … But you've never even kissed me. Never even tried. You're just saying this to make me have second thoughts about Aidan, aren't you? You don't really want me. But you don't want him to have me either. What is wrong with you?'

Simon glared at her. 'What's wrong with me? I'll tell you what's wrong with me. I'm in love with a woman who isn't in love with me. I'm in love with a woman who thinks she loves someone else. I'm in love with a woman who drives me nuts, but who it seems I can't live without. I'm in love with the wrong bloody woman. That's what's wrong with me. And no, I don't want him to have you because I want you. I want you so badly sometimes, I get dizzy just thinking about it. You're right, I don't like change. I was scared if things changed between us I might lose you forever. But the way things are going, that will probably happen anyway. And as for never kissing you, well, at least that's one thing I can change.'

She had no time to digest his words; he pulled her against his hard, athletic body, wrapped strong arms around her and kissed her with a passion she had never imagined he had.

It must have shocked him as much as it shocked her because before she had time to respond, he let her go, so unexpectedly that she had to grab the nearby lamppost to steady herself.

He walked away so fast that it turned into a jog and then he was running. Running away from her as if his life depended on it. And she couldn't even whisper his name, let alone call after him.

Chapter Thirty-Six

The ringing in Ali's ears as she leant against the lamppost suddenly stopped, and then began again. The third time it happened, she realised it was her phone.

She didn't want to speak to anyone until she had regained her composure, but it could be her mum, or her dad. Or it could be Aidan, to let her know he was OK. Not that she cared about Aidan at this moment in time. She didn't even care about her mum or dad for that matter. All she could think about, all she cared about was Simon and that amazing kiss.

Several beeps announced her phone had received some texts, and sighing inwardly, she took it from her bag and glanced at the screen. It was from Jules, and she sounded desperate if the, 'where the hell are you? For Christ's sake call me. ASAP!' was anything to go by.

Worried about her friend, Ali immediately phoned Jules.

'What's happened, Jules? Are you OK?'

'No, I'm bloody well not. Where are you? I've been calling you for ages. It's a disaster. Everything's a sodding disaster. I don't know what to do. It's over. It has to be. The whole thing's a complete mess. Well, say something, will you? I need your advice. I'm going bloody mad here.'

'Tell me what's wrong. Where are you?'

'I'm at the flat. I've just got back. Why didn't he tell me before now? Why did he leave it so late? Why did he even ask me to marry him, if all the time he felt like that?'

Ali pushed herself away from the lamppost and started running towards Jules' flat. 'Bruce, you mean? What's happened? What's he said? I'm on my way. I'll be there in just a minute. I'm only around the corner.'

'Hurry up. I'll explode if I don't talk to someone soon.'

Ali reached the flat in record time and, using the spare key that Jules had given her, let herself in, taking the stairs two at a time and bursting into the living room, gasping for breath. Jules ran to her and collapsed into her arms, sobbing on Ali's shoulder.

'I can't believe it. I want to hate him, but I can't.'

Ali let her cry for a moment before gently easing her away and leading her to the sofa, shoving a pile of bridal magazines onto the floor so that she and Jules could sit.

'Now tell me what has happened. What is this all about?'

Jules sniffed and wiped her eyes with the back of her hand. 'Purple. Bruce hates the colour purple.'

Ali stared at her friend, blinking as she tried to comprehend the meaning of those words.

'Purple? That's it? There's nothing else? That's why you're so upset? Because your fiancé doesn't like purple?' Ali wanted to laugh, but from the incredulous look on Jules' face, that clearly wouldn't help matters.

'You sound as if you don't think it's serious,' Jules said, glowering at Ali. 'He hates purple. Hates it.'

Ali squeezed Jules' hands in hers. 'Yes, but does that matter? It's a colour. I thought he'd told you he'd had an affair or something. Or was gay, and not really into women at all. Although as I've known him all my life, I know that isn't true.'

'Does it matter? Of course it matters. And it's worse than an affair. An affair I could live with. Purple, I can't live without. Don't you see? Don't you get it? Look!' She threw her arm in the air drawing Ali's attention to the room. 'Purple. Everywhere. The walls, the furniture, soft furnishings. My salon downstairs. Jesus, even my hair is purple. My fiancé even hates my hair. How can I spend my life with a man who hates my favourite colour? It's impossible.'

'OK,' Ali said, getting to her feet. 'He clearly doesn't hate your hair, and I don't believe he hates the colour purple, either. He wouldn't have been able to date you, come to the salon to see you, spend so many nights in this flat, if he really despised it that much. I'm going to open a bottle of wine, and we're going to sit and discuss this sensibly.' She went into the kitchen, grabbed a bottle of white wine from the fridge and glasses from the cupboard and returned to find Jules staring at the purple cushion now sitting on her lap.

'Perhaps you're right,' Jules said, looking up as Ali poured the wine and handed Jules a glass. 'Perhaps this isn't about purple at all. Perhaps he's decided he doesn't want to marry me. That he doesn't love me enough.'

'He loves you. That's obvious. And I'm sure he wants to marry you. I think it's probably the usual story.'

'What story?'

'Cold feet.'

'My feet aren't cold. He always complains how hot they are. Neither are his. Oh. You didn't mean our actual feet.'

'No.' Ali smiled. 'I didn't.'

'So what happens now? What am I supposed to do? When we got back home, I told him to get lost. I said I never wanted to see him again. I told him there was clearly something wrong with him if he didn't like purple.'

'That doesn't matter. May I ask you a question without you biting my head off?'

Jules shrugged.

'Marriage means compromise. Are you prepared to compromise? I mean, your salon is where you work and that should be any colour you want because Bruce doesn't have to spend any time there, except perhaps a few minutes every so often. But once you're married, you'll be moving into the house you're currently buying together. Unlike this flat, it won't be just your choice of decoration. It'll be a shared choice. That means less purple. As little as possible, in fact. I'm your best friend and you know I love you, but I have to be honest, purple isn't my favourite colour either. That doesn't mean I love you less. It simply means I don't love purple. You wouldn't end our friendship because I told you that. Would you?'

Jules seemed to need a moment to consider that.

'No. No I wouldn't.'

'So why do you need to end your relationship? I know you'll be spending more time with Bruce than you spend with me, but still, surely there's a colour you both like? What about gold? Does Bruce hate gold?'

'Not likely. He's got a gold watch. He buys me gold jewellery. There're gold-plated taps in his bathroom.'

'Well, there you are then. Have more gold. And perhaps a paler shade of purple might not be such problem for him. Lilac, for example. That's a sort of purple and it goes just as well with gold.'

Jules visibly brightened. 'You're right. So what should I do? Should I see if he calls me? Or should I call him?'

'Someone's got to make the first move, so why not you? I'll tell you exactly what you should do. You should phone him right now. Find out if he's at home. And go straight round and tell him how much you love him. Then tell him that you want to choose the colours of your new house together and that you'll be happy if you can have a couple of purple cushions, or something.'

'Just cushions?' Jules looked worried. 'OK. I can do this. You're right.' She emptied her glass and held it out for a refill, pressing Bruce's number on her phone with her other hand.

'Bruce, where are you?' she asked when he answered. 'On your way here?' She glanced at Ali. 'Yes. I love you too.' Her anxious look turned into a smile. 'I'm sorry, too. I'll see you very soon.'

Ali stood up. 'I think that's my cue to leave.'

Jules rang off and jumped to her feet, throwing her arms around Ali. 'You're the best friend in the world. Oh God. I haven't asked about your mum. Or Aidan. Or anything. Is everything OK?'

Ali kissed Jules on the cheek. 'Everything is fine,' she lied. 'Call me tomorrow and tell me how it went.'

Chapter Thirty-Seven

Simon was clearly avoiding Ali. All her calls went to voicemail and her texts went unanswered. He wouldn't even open the front door to her, no matter how hard she knocked or how long she kept her finger pressed on the doorbell. He hadn't responded to the note she had slipped through his letterbox, asking him to call her as soon as he could, and all her emails were returned marked 'Simon Hart is away from his desk at present but will respond to emails on his return.' He hadn't even turned up at the centre to help out, as he always did in the holidays, but Grace said that she had spoken to him and he had said he would be away for a few days.

The man was definitely a jerk. How could anyone tell someone that they love them, kiss them so passionately that they nearly blow that person's mind and then disappear as if in a puff of smoke? It didn't make any sense. But then nothing about this situation made any sense. At least not to Ali.

Almost two weeks had passed since he'd kissed her, and no matter what she did, or where she went, she couldn't get the twerp out of her thoughts. Even Aidan's continued flirting wasn't having any effect. He kept buzzing around her like that damned bee. If only she could swat him away so easily. Mind you, she wouldn't want him to turn on her and bite her on her neck, or anywhere else for that matter, so it was probably just as well.

The first few days, Aidan had simply phoned to try and fix another date, but Ali's various excuses were obviously wearing thin. By the end of that week, his requests were made in person, accompanied by flowers, chocolates, a bottle of champagne. At the start of the second week, he had upped his game. He brought her a very pretty necklace with, curiously enough, a black and gold metallic bumblebee charm attached. She had accepted the flowers graciously, and shared the chocolates and champagne with the staff, but she had to decline the lovely necklace, using as an excuse, that sadly, she was allergic to costume jewellery.

'I'm beginning to think you're trying to send me a message,' Aidan said, still holding the necklace out to her in its beautiful pale blue box. 'And it isn't costume jewellery. The chain is gold, and the bee is gold and jet.'

'Gold?' Ali swallowed hard and began rearranging papers on her desk. 'Then I definitely can't accept it.'

'Why not?' His tone indicated his displeasure.

'Because we don't have that sort of relationship.'

'We could have. We should have. The third attempt, remember? Nothing's changed on my part. Has something changed on yours?'

How could she tell him that there was a very strong possibility that she had fallen in love with her best friend? Was that completely true? Had she always been a little in love with Simon without recognising it as that sort of love?

'There's been a lot going on. I haven't really had time to think about it. This week's been busy here and Sim… I mean … we're short-staffed because one of our volunteers has let us down. Plus, I'm helping Jules re-plan her wedding. She's no longer having purple and gold, but gold and white instead. Everything's got to be cancelled and reordered. And then there's Bonnie and Bertie's wedding to arrange. That's taking up a lot more of my time than I anticipated.'

'Bonnie and Bertie?'

'Gertie's dogs.'

Aidan rolled his eyes. 'Surely Tabitha could help with that? Now that she and Tom have reconciled and have both resigned from their jobs – which still amazes me, I have to say. She must have plenty of free time on her hands to assist with her mother's ridiculous whims.'

Ali glowered at him. 'They aren't ridiculous. Bonnie and Bertie mean a great deal to all of us.

We're all looking forward to the wedding this weekend, especially as it's also Mum and Dad's wedding anniversary, and they're having a party at the house with marquees in the garden. Mum's busy organising that, which is something else I'm helping with, and I'm thrilled to bits, of course. Sunday is going to be a truly wonderful day. We're starting off at nine, with a wedding breakfast for Bonnie and Bertie, at Josie's.'

'That American diner on the hill?'

'Yes. Dogs are allowed on the decking and the forecast for the weekend is glorious weather and soaring temperatures. You can come if you want. Everyone's invited.'

Why had she said that? Did she want him there? What if Simon showed up? Now she was being ridiculous. Simon was avoiding her, so he would hardly want to attend Bonnie and Bertie's wedding breakfast, or her mum and dad's anniversary party, even though he had been invited to both. She had hand delivered the invitations herself although she had had to put them through the letterbox as he wasn't at home, according to Grace.

'To a dogs' wedding breakfast?' Aidan's scowl suddenly became a smile. 'That actually sounds like fun. I'd love to come. Does the invitation extend to your parents' party too?'

Ali nodded. What else could she do?

'Great. Then I'll leave you in peace because you're obviously very busy. And I'll see you on

Sunday morning, bright and early. Hopefully, wearing this. And later, hopefully wearing nothing else, but this.' He winked at her and placed the pale blue box on the pile of papers in front of her.

'Aidan, I can't. I can't accept this.'

He smiled and walked away. 'You can. And you will.'

She watched him go, closed the lid of the box and put it to one side. 'I damn well won't, you know.'

Chapter Thirty-Eight

Ali leant back in the purple chair as Daisy slathered her hair in shampoo and Jules put the finishing touches to Sasha's wash and blow-dry.

'Now if you hate it, I can change you back to blonde.' Jules said, directing her comment to Ali.

'No. That previous colour made me realise, I can be any colour I want. And now I want to be ginger, with gold and purple highlights. And we need to try out the colour in plenty of time, now that you've brought your wedding forward to September.'

'We're going to go to church more often,' Jules said. 'Bruce and I discussed it. At least four times a year now, instead of just Christmas Eve. That vicar really is lovely, and so helpful, too. And we were lucky to get the cancellation. I wonder what that couple rowed about to make them break up. I hope they sort it out and get back together. But they can't have their wedding date back if they do.'

'I love the new invitations,' Sasha said. 'That white and gold with the one purple flower embossed through the middle of it, is really beautiful.'

Jules smiled. 'And I have to admit that the white and gold wedding dress, with the purple sash and the purple and orange bouquet looks far more beautiful than the purple and gold dress did. My flat even looks better since Bruce painted three of the walls pale lilac, and this salon looks so much brighter now that I've replaced the wallpaper with white and gold. I've had lots of positive feedback from my clients too.'

'Everything seems to be working out wonderfully, doesn't it?' Sasha said as Ali got up from the purple chair at the basin and joined them at the row of once purple chairs, now replaced by white imitation leather ones, in front of the wall of mirrors. 'Your parents are like newlyweds. Jules has, thankfully, let go of her obsession with purple and become much more light-hearted in the process.'

'Oi! I was always light-hearted. And I still love purple. It's just that I now love some other colours too.'

Sasha grinned. 'And you bringing your wedding date forward when you heard of the cancellation worked out brilliantly for me and John. Neither of us wanted to wait until next year, and December suits us perfectly.'

Jules grabbed her handheld mirror and held it behind Sasha's head, to enable Sasha to see her hair in the reflection. 'I can't wait until Bonnie and Bertie's wedding tomorrow.' She glanced at Ali. 'Have you decided what you're wearing?'

Ali shrugged, as Daisy patted her hair dry with a towel. 'Not yet. I bought a gorgeous pale blue dress via the internet a couple of weeks ago. It's got thin navy-blue straps, a low-cut – but not too low – navy trimmed, snug fitting bodice, and a pale blue flowing skirt with a navy, gossamer, petticoat-thing beneath. I love it. The problem is my pale blue sandals will kill me if I wear them for several hours again, and my navy-blue sandals are equally as high. But low-heeled sandals don't do the dress justice, so I'm not sure what to do.'

'Simple,' Sasha said. 'Wear the navy-blue ones, and get Simon to give you a piggyback everywhere.'

Ali frowned at her. 'I don't think Simon's coming. I haven't heard a word from him since he kissed me and ran off.'

'Simon kissed you?' Daisy asked, in a dreamlike manner. 'You're so lucky. Simon Hart is gorgeous.'

'You fancy Simon?'

Daisy nodded and Sasha and Jules tutted.

'Everyone fancies Simon,' Sasha said. 'Everyone except you, that is. Although since he kissed you, you seem to have changed your tune. I couldn't believe that when you told us.'

'I could,' Jules said. 'And it's about bloody time. Although why the stupid twit then went away on holiday is beyond me.'

'Did he go away?' Daisy asked. 'Only if he did, he's back. I saw him less than an hour ago. He was talking to your dad, Ali.'

The door of the salon burst open and Sheila Clutterdrew headed straight for them like a ballistic missile. 'Oh my goodness. Have you heard the news? I can't believe it. I phoned my sister right away. It's a miracle. We're saved. You must tell Ali. Oh! You're here. You must be delighted. And your staff. It's wonderful. Simply wonderful. Of course, it isn't over yet. But it will be. They haven't got a leg to stand on. I must say Jules, I love what you've done with the salon. The colours are simply beautiful. Must run. Got to spread the word.'

'Er, Sheila, babe,' Jules said, in a slightly bored tone. 'You haven't told us the news.'

'Haven't I? Oh dear.'

'Daisy. Would you open a bottle of wine, please?' Jules asked. 'I'm sure Sheila has time for a glass, and any excuse is good enough for us.'

'That be wonderful, dear,' Sheila said, plonking herself down in a chair and smiling.

'The news, Sheila?' Jules added.

'Oh yes. The news. There's been opposition to that pre-planning application thing I told you about. And not just from us. All sorts of organisations are involved. Daphne, from the local paper told me. You know that little copse the other side of Josie's diner where some of the trees go down to the river? Ancient woodland, apparently. Protected. Right where they want their road to go. And that's not all. They don't even own all the land. Landlocked or something. There's an area of land all around the centre which isn't owned by them. There's a right of way, but it's only granted to the centre on condition it stays as it is. They can't develop it. Not without that land. Unless they bring everyone in by boat.' Sheila waved a piece of paper she had been holding. 'I've written it down. Didn't want to get it wrong.'

Ali, Jules, Sasha and Daisy all stared from one to the other and back at Sheila, as Daisy handed around the glasses of wine.

'So, what you're telling us,' Ali said, taking hers, 'is that the centre has to remain a water sports centre, otherwise the right of way lapses? But surely they could buy that land?'

'Tried to. The owners won't sell. The solicitors were negligent. Wouldn't want to be in their shoes. They should have bought that land when they bought the centre, but someone made a mistake.' Sheila gulped down her wine. 'A body needed that. Bless you, Jules. Must run. More people to tell. See you at the wedding breakfast tomorrow.' She struggled out of the chair and waddled out of the salon, waving as she did so.

'Well, babe,' Jules said, knocking back her wine. 'Aidan's not going to be in a good mood tomorrow, is he? Although as he told you it was all a mistake in the first place, perhaps it won't make any difference.'

'Mistake, my arse,' Sasha said. 'Don't look at me like that. I don't believe it for a minute. I never did. Men like the Rourkes don't buy water sports centres like ours unless they want to turn them into posh clubs, or redevelop the land they're on. There's obviously more money in redevelopment, but if they can't do that, the posh club will have to do.'

'I hope not,' Ali said. 'I couldn't bear that. Assuming I'd still have a job. I know the centre needs to be more profitable, but people love it the way it is. Schools and children's groups can't afford extortionate fees. I hope there's something we can do to stop it. If only Mum and Dad were millionaires.'

'We could all club together,' Jules said. 'You know, like those co-operative thingies. I've read about them. All the locals get together and buy whatever it is they want to save.'

Sasha shook her head. 'I don't think anyone around here has got enough money to buy something owned by the Rourkes. I'm sure they got the centre for a song, but I bet it'll need a full-blown opera to buy it from them.'

Chapter Thirty-Nine

Simon may be back – and according to Daisy, he was – but he still wasn't taking Ali's calls. Or answering her texts. And he hadn't opened the door last night when she had gone to his house after leaving Shimmering Scissors Hair and Beauty. She was helping her mum all evening, so she couldn't go around again, but the five text messages and two voicemails she had left had all met with the same response. Silence.

At least she would be seeing him at the wedding breakfast, the church and her parents' garden party, because according to her mum and Gertie, Simon had responded to all three invitations in the affirmative. He had even apologised for his late response, using the excuse of a few days away. That had annoyed her all the more. A few days, indeed. Almost two weeks, more like.

Ali finished helping Gertie put Bonnie's dress on, easing her tiny paws into the satin and lace sleeves. The dear little dog actually seemed as excited as any bride might be on their wedding day.

Excited? What was she thinking? What was so exciting about getting married, for goodness sake? When so many marriages ended in divorce, statistically speaking, who would want to take a chance on that?

Her mum would. She was even talking about her and Tom renewing their vows. And Sasha would. She was so excited, that she had jumped at the chance of taking the wedding date Jules and Bruce had vacated. And Jules would, obviously. Not only had she brought the wedding forward, she had even changed the colour scheme to please her fiancé, Bruce. Even little Bonnie here, was keen.

Was Ali the only person with an aversion to marriage? And did she even really feel that way? Last night she had a dream that today was her wedding breakfast. Hers and Simon's. How ridiculous was that? But he had said he loved her. And then he disappeared for almost two weeks without a word. Not one word. Let alone those three little words that always meant so much.

'The car's here, my angel.' Gertie adjusted her hat and smiled at Ali. 'You make a beautiful bridesmaid. Or dogsmaid, should that be? Especially with your new hair colour. I thought the last colour suited you, but the ginger, purple and gold really bring out the colour of your eyes. I hope someone appreciates it. Now let's get on. You carry Bonnie in her wedding basket. I'll carry Bertie in his.'

Even this didn't seem crazy any more, and Ali did as Gertie asked, linking her arm through Gertie's and walking together towards the car. The chauffeur of the limousine helped them in and didn't bat an eyelid at his unusually dressed passengers. He had probably seen it all before. They arrived at Josie's within minutes and it was a sight to behold. There was bunting, balloons, and congratulatory banners everywhere she looked. Guests already mingled inside, dressed in finery just as they would when attending any wedding. Some were outside on the deck where gentle breezes lifted the hems of women's skirts and ruffled the men's hair.

'I think we're going to have a wonderful day, don't you, Ali-ba-ba?'

'I think you're right,' Ali replied, getting out of the car and helping her gran, as the chauffeur held the baskets containing Bonnie and Bertie. 'The weather's perfect. The decorations are superb. We know the food will be excellent. The guests have all arrived and are looking happy. There's birdsong and music and laughter in the air. What more could any bride want on her wedding day?'

Dear God. Was she really feeling tearful? At a dogs' wedding?

'To know she was marrying the right man,' Gertie said. 'It takes two to tango, my angel, and marriage is definitely a dance. Or to put it in a more appropriate manner: 'It takes two to paddle a canoe along the river of wedded bliss. Make sure you have the right man in your canoe, and that you're both paddling in the same direction. You can ride any rapids if you are. Now come along. We have guests waiting.'

Ali smiled as Gertie took Bertie and his basket from the chauffeur and handed Bonnie and her basket to Ali.

A cheer went up amongst the guests as the wedding party approached the door to the Shimmering River Diner, and Mendelssohn's Wedding March boomed out from inside. The interior of the diner was decorated as exquisitely as the outside and Ali glanced around at the various tables and the people standing beside them, clapping. She smiled at some; nodded and smiled at others. Waved and said hello to several, as they made their way to the main table outside on the deck.

The sight of it took Ali's breath away. Four posts – two each end – held a white canopy trimmed with wild flowers, and sunflowers stood in ribbon-wrapped pots beside the posts. On the table sat little white baskets, similar but miniatures of the ones carrying Bonnie and Bertie at the moment. They were filled with colourful confetti in the shape of tiny bones. Cutlery glistened in the sunlight and glasses gleamed. Everything looked perfect. And then, she saw him – and he took her breath away. He was standing beside the table, dressed in a light grey morning suit, like a groom waiting for his bride, and she fought the urge to run to him as he slowly met her eyes.

'Hello, Simon,' she said, when she eventually drew level with him.

'Hello, Ali,' he replied.

'Well,' Gertie said, after they had stared at one another for several seconds. 'Now that you two have got that warm welcome over with, let's sit, shall we? I'm as hungry as a wolf and as dry as a desert.'

'Ali, darling,' Tabitha said, appearing by Ali's side from amongst the crowd. 'You look absolutely gorgeous, doesn't she, Tom?'

Tom nodded, his arm firmly wrapped around Tabitha's waist. 'You both do,' he replied. 'And so do Bonnie and Bertie, I'm astonished to admit. You too, Gertie.'

Gertie smiled. 'Let's get this wedding breakfast started. The vicar won't wait, you know, and then there's a wedding anniversary bash to attend. Who's got the champagne?'

'Right here, Gertie,' Josie said, carrying an ice bucket and a magnum of the stuff. 'There's more where this came from, so don't you fret.'

'I'm not,' Gertie said. 'I'm going to have a good time.'

Ali looked around at the throng of happy guests and then looked back at Simon and her smile slid from her face. He didn't look happy.

'If you're looking for Aidan, I think you'll be disappointed. I'm sorry, Ali, but I don't think he's coming.'

'I wasn't. I was looking at all the guests. Everyone's so bright and cheerful. Everyone except you, that is. You look like a fish out of water.'

'I haven't got much to smile about. But I'm not being miserable. I wouldn't dream of ruining this special day by being down in the dumps.'

She looked him up and down. 'Where did you get that tan?'

'It's summer. Skin tans in the sun, you know.'

'Don't be sarcastic. You've been away.'

'I'm surprised you noticed.'

'Grace told me.'

'Ah. That explains it. Excuse me.' He walked away and disappeared into the crowd.

Ali chased after him but couldn't see him in the crush. She searched everywhere for several minutes, wondering if he'd left, until finally she saw him. He was sitting inside. In what she was certain was the booth they had occupied the last time they were here together.

She marched inside and plonked herself down opposite him. 'Why are you sitting in here on such a glorious day?'

'What concern is that of yours?'

'Simon. Stop behaving like a twerp. Don't you think we should talk?'

'What is there to talk about?'

Her eyes opened wide. 'What is there to talk about? Well, lots of things. About the centre and what can be done to save it. It concerns you just as much as it does me, you know. And then there's the question of who owns this mysterious piece of land. You must've heard about what's going on, even if you've just got back from wherever it is you disappeared to. And then there's the issue of whether or not there's any chance of the village clubbing together and purchasing the land back from the Rourkes. And that's just for starters.'

'Hasn't your boyfriend told you? Or did he vanish without a word? You don't have to do anything to save the centre. It's already saved. And the Rourkes won't own it for very much longer. I can assure you of that.'

'What? Firstly, if you're referring to Aidan – which you obviously are – he's not my boyfriend. He never really was. Yes, I fancied him. Yes, I was a little infatuated with him. But I didn't love him, I haven't had sex with him, and I couldn't care less if I never see him again. What do you mean, the centre's already saved? Who by? When? I only heard all this yesterday. And what makes you so sure they're going to sell? Oh my God! You're not going to tell me that it's you who owns that piece of land and you've kept it a secret from me for all these years!'

He tilted his head to one side and the merest hint of a smile curved his lips. 'No, I'm not.'

Ali let out the breath she was holding.

'Josie and I own it, via a company she and my dad set up, many, many years ago.'

'What?'

'The Rourkes' lawyers really messed up. They'll be sued for a fortune, I don't doubt. But anyway, without our piece of land, no development can go ahead. And Josie and I will never sell it. No matter how much we're offered. The Rourkes can't even expand the centre because the deed granting rights of way is pretty restrictive. They can't encroach on our land with any building whatsoever. Our land completely surrounds the centre, so it doesn't give them much scope. They can retain the centre and continue as it is, but I can't see them doing that. There's no money in it for them, and the Rourkes are all about the money. Josie and I, and another local company have made them an offer. A fairly good one, all things considered. I'm pretty sure they'll take it.'

Ali stared at him with her mouth open.

'Why didn't you tell me any of this, Simon?'

He shrugged. 'Because it's not important. Well, it is now, but it wasn't. We didn't know that the centre was being sold, otherwise we would've bought it at the time, and then I would've told you.' He grinned. 'Partly because then I would've been your boss. Sort of. That was the one sensible thing Aidan did. Make you manager. That's what we would've done. But I didn't tell you because money isn't everything, Ali. Why does it matter what I own or don't own? It doesn't change who I am, or what I think or feel. I'm a Maths teacher, who loves messing around on the water.' He shrugged again and rested his forearms on the table.

Ali shook her head. 'I'm not sure I can take all this in. You might need to explain it all to me again sometime. But there's something else we should discuss.'

'What's that?'

'Simon.' She slapped his forearm with her hand. 'The things you said before you disappeared. The things you did.'

He looked confused.

'That kiss, you twerp. And the fact that you said you loved me.'

His eyes narrowed and he stared into hers. 'As far as the kiss is concerned, there's not very much to talk about, is there? Other than the fact that I'd give anything to do it again. And I do love you, Ali. I suspect I always have. I've simply been too much of a jerk to realise it. But I know you don't feel the same, so it's clearly my problem and I'll have to learn to deal with it. The best way for me to do that, is for me to avoid seeing you, or talking to you, or having anything to do with you, as much as possible, that is.'

'It's my problem too, if it means I'll hardly ever see you.' She leant forward and smiled as the cheers and laughter and music grew louder outside. 'But I think I have the solution to both our problems. Marry me, Simon. It makes perfect sense.'

He blinked several times and his mouth fell open.

'That's not funny, Ali,' he finally said.

'It wasn't meant to be. You may be a twerp, but I love you. I really, really love you. I think I always have. I was just too much of a stubborn fool to see it. But if you've got an aversion to marriage, we could simply live together. I don't care what we do, as long as I'm with you.'

A bee buzzed around them and bashed its head against the glass. Simon stood, opened the window further than it was, and let the bee out. Then suddenly he burst out laughing – a cheery laugh, full of warmth and fun and even a little passion.

'Me? Have an aversion to marriage? You're the one who hates the very thought of it.'

'Apparently not, it seems. Provided it's to you.' She stood up and walked around the table to stand in front of him. 'In fact, I rather like the thought of it. I've been thinking of very little else for almost two weeks. Now about that kiss.'

'Forget that kiss,' he said, pulling her into his arms. This is the kiss we're both going to remember for the rest of our married lives. And then we have a wedding breakfast and a wedding to attend.' His lips came slowly towards hers.

'And an anniversary party,' she mumbled, a second before he kissed her.

She suddenly pulled away from him. 'Wait. Did you say, "married lives"?'

He nodded. 'Uh-huh. As you said, it is the answer to all our problems. Living together just wouldn't work for me.' He grinned and winked at her. 'And I'm not sure my mum would like it. It has to be marriage. It really is the only solution.'

'I completely agree,' Ali said, smiling at him as she wrapped her arms around his neck. 'I don't understand what some people have against marriage. I want to be married. I want to be your wife. And the sooner the better, I think.'

A Note From Emily

Thank you for reading this book. I hope you enjoyed reading it as much as I enjoyed writing it. A little piece of my heart goes into all of my books and when I send them on their way, I really hope they bring a smile to someone's face. If this book made you smile, or gave you a few pleasant hours of relaxation, I'd love to hear from you, via social media, on your blog if you have one, or by email. I'd be incredibly grateful if you have a minute or two to post a review. Just a line will do, and a kind review makes such a difference to my day – to any author's day. Huge thanks to those of you who are happy to do so, and for your lovely comments and support on social media. Thank you. A writer's life can be lonely at times. Sharing a virtual cup of coffee or a glass of wine, or exchanging a few friendly words on Facebook, Twitter or Instagram is so much fun.

You might like to join my Readers' Club by signing up for my newsletter. It's absolutely free, your email address is safe with me and I won't bombard you, I promise. You can enter my competitions and enjoy some giveaways. In addition to that, there's my author page on Facebook but there's also a new Facebook group and I'm very excited about it. You can chat with me and with other readers and get access to my book news, snippets from my daily life, early extracts from my books and lots more besides. Details are on the 'For You' page of my website. You'll find all my contact links in the Contact section following this.

I'm probably working on my next book right now. Let's see where my characters take us this time. Hope to chat with you soon.

To see details of my other books, please go to the books page on my website or scan the QR code, below. www.emilyharvale.com/books.

***

Scan the code above to see Emily's books on Amazon

To read about me, my books, my work in progress and competitions, freebies, or to contact me, pop over to my website www.emilyharvale.com. To be the first to hear about new releases and other news, you can subscribe to my Readers' Club newsletter via the 'Sign me up' box.

Or come and say 'Hello' on Facebook, Twitter or Instagram. Hope to chat with you soon.

17424803R00162

Printed in Great Britain
by Amazon